MEASURE OF DAYS

MEASURE OF DAYS

SOPHY LAYZELL

The Book Guild Ltd

First published in Great Britain in 2020 by
The Book Guild Ltd
9 Priory Business Park
Wistow Road, Kibworth
Leicestershire, LE8 0RX
Freephone: 0800 999 2982
www.bookguild.co.uk
Email: info@bookguild.co.uk
Twitter: @bookguild

Typeset in 12pt Adobe Jenson Pro

Printed and bound by CPI Group (UK) Ltd, Croydon, CR0 4YY

ISBN 978 1913208 721

British Library Cataloguing in Publication Data.

A catalogue record for this book is available from the British Library.

Dedicated to my daughter Amelia,
who I love beyond words.

"And this shall be the plague...
their flesh shall dissolve while they stand on their feet,
their eyes shall dissolve in their sockets,
and their tongues shall dissolve in their mouths."

Zech. 14:12-15

DETER

The second time that Deter regained consciousness, the sharp, acrid smell of ammonia was still there.

This time, instead of darkness, the room was ablaze with light. It was a small room, the walls subdued, grimy ochre with cracked lines and a huge stain on the ceiling left over from a water leak above. Three portable builder's work lights, with a fourth shining right at her bed, lit the room. Deter had never been anywhere like it before, as her life so far had been spent in cosseted luxury. She looked around cautiously, her heart beating increasingly loud, almost as though it were lodged in her ears. Fear rising, she tried not to move, peering beneath half-closed lids to try and assess the situation. Where was she? How did she get here? What happened to her friends? She could sense a presence behind her, and that someone moved to stand next to her. It was a young man wearing plastic gloves and an anxious expression. He tidied some vials and equipment into a box and coughed nervously as he focussed on his task.

"Oh, you're awake." He paused. "I hope you're not in too much pain?"

He looked at her kindly, genuinely concerned, and Deter knew there was something trustworthy about him. She lifted her arms, testing her movements and, trying to sit up: "I don't know, I think I'm OK."

He must be a doctor, she thought woozily, as she lay back down, grimacing with pain, feeling the ache of bruising down her left side. She knew something had happened, but she couldn't remember what. Her head felt it was going to explode. She tried to make herself focus, as she knew she had to make a huge effort to find out what was going on. If Amery were here, she'd tell her to dig deep; after all, 'nothing comes from nothing', as she was always telling her. Thinking of Amery gave her a sharp pain in her chest. Her guardian would be so worried about her. She wanted to shut her eyes and ignore this boy, but she also wanted answers, so she braced herself and sat up.

"Where am I? What's happening?"

Hugo had given Lincoln no guidance on what the Immune was to be told, so Lincoln hesitated before saying, "Well, it's a complicated but important story."

Judging by his medical role and his slight build, she could sense he wasn't one of the men who had attacked her. He seemed almost apologetic to be here. She pressed on, wanting to keep him talking. "Go on, it doesn't look as though I'm going anywhere."

Deter knew that it was important to build up as much detail about her situation as possible. She suspected that she had been kidnapped. Ever since she had been young this had been Amery's greatest fear, and her guardian had repeatedly reinforced the importance of gathering information. DNA under the fingernails was useful, so scratch and gouge if you get the chance. Be observant; take in their physical details, their clothes and their accents. The problem was, she could remember very little, as it had all happened so fast, but Deter had absolute faith that Amery would be tracking her down and a ransom would be paid. She just had to make sure she stayed safe until then.

"Where's Amery?"

"Er… Amery?"

"She's my guardian. She was with me. We were on our way out of state."

"No idea." Lincoln snapped the box shut and turned to leave. He couldn't leave; he hadn't told her anything.

Deter leant forward anxiously. "What about my friends? Where are they? Have you captured them too?"

"Again… no idea what you're talking about." Lincoln started walking towards the door.

She forced herself upright. "So, how much are you asking?" That was a deliberate challenge and Deter could see that the question had thrown him.

"How much for what?" He turned to look at her.

"Me, of course. I'm afraid I've never been kidnapped before so I'm not sure what the current asking price for heiresses is."

Heiresses? Lincoln raised his eyebrows. *She really doesn't know anything!* Money would be useful to the Faction; they hadn't thought of asking the Establishment for a ransom, but money was nothing compared to her priceless immune system.

"Deter—" he began.

"And how do you know my name?" she interrupted. "I have no idea who you are, or where I am."

Lincoln wasn't sure what it was that made him feel he ought to tell her. It certainly wasn't her imperious tone. Possibly it was the open and trusting way she looked at him. Or it could be that he felt guilty. After all, he'd played his part in getting her here, and he had just examined her without her consent while she was passed out, and that made him feel uncomfortable. She had a perfect body, apart from the bruises that he had been partially responsible for inflicting. But she was brave and sparky. The jealousy he had felt before he met her was overtaken by admiration and also a slight possessiveness. If he was going to be honest with himself, he also thought she was the most beautiful person he had ever seen.

"My name is Lincoln. You are held by a pressure group called the Faction. We campaign for better governance and alternative solutions to the FED crisis." He held up his hand as she was about to interrupt. "I appreciate you might know nothing about us, the Faction, but just understand that you are special to us. Not because you offer a chance of wealth but because you are immune to the terrible Flesh-Eating Disease, FED. We need your DNA to help create a vaccine, as it's the only way to save us from eventual extinction. As you know, the Establishment has complete power and can't or won't create one. We believe we can. I'm so sorry, but in order to do that, we need you. That's why you're here."

A flesh-eating disease? She had never heard of such a thing. They looked at each other in silence, while she tried to absorb what he had just told her.

"I don't believe you," Deter finally said flatly, glaring at him. He seemed completely serious, but she had never even heard of FED. Surely she would know about something so devastating, so intrinsic to society. It would be on the news all the time, wouldn't it? She knew that Amery protected her from unpleasant things, but this should be common knowledge. It suddenly dawned on her that she wasn't dealing with a straightforward kidnapper. This was a deluded psychopath. Just her luck!

"I've lived in New York all my life and neither my friends nor I have ever heard of any of this. FED? What a load of rubbish! Our biggest concern is terrorism, which is something you seem dangerously close to."

He looked so surprised Deter stopped feeling angry and stared at him. What was happening?

It was now Lincoln's turn to stare at her, thinking her words through. A terrorist? That was a strong word and not one he associated with himself. There was so much to explain that he didn't know where to start. Explaining about their cause, their plans, the history of FED, it felt such a huge responsibility. Part of him didn't feel this burden was his, but he felt guilty about the part he was playing. Also, he knew it would better coming from him than Hugo or Angus, so reluctantly he continued, "I can only tell you what I know. How can you not have heard of FED? It's literally the only thing that matters in the world right now." He paused, waiting for her permission.

"Go on." Her voice had gone faint and husky.

"Well, no one is quite sure how FED started, but this particular strain first became known about eighty years ago. It's a bacterium that has always existed and affected the population sporadically, but in rare and isolated incidences. The bacteria could live on healthy people's skin but not affect them, flaring up after a virus or severe wound. But then it began to evolve into a virulent strain that causes the body's immune system to destroy its own tissue incredibly quickly and it's become contagious. It is, however, unpredictable, and some people don't contract it for years while others are affected when they are very young." He paused, checking she was taking this information in. Stepping forward towards her, he relaxed a little and continued, "They think they can trace the first outbreak of FED to Dartmoor ponies in the south-west of England. There is evidence that it started there, and that wounds from gorse bushes accelerated the spread to the human population.

"It spread slowly at first but transmuted to become contagious within a decade. Small, infected communities put themselves into quarantine, while uninfected ones also cut themselves off.

"It became a universal fight and all medical research was put on hold as all resources were focussed on finding a cure. Leading and coordinating this was a group of prominent medical scientists who united governments in this common battle. They called themselves the Establishment."

"But you said they have a cure now."

"Yes, they discovered it twenty years ago."

"So... what's the problem?"

He winced, wanting to spare her the details. "It's not the solution that we thought it was."

They sat in silence for a while as Deter tried to process everything she'd just been told. It was shocking and yet somehow, she could feel the truth behind the boy's words. Why would he lie?

"But, what about you? You look fine. So does everyone else in New York that I've ever seen. Jameson, Amery, Jenny and Padma."

"We might look fine but every diseased part of us has probably been replaced."

"Replaced with what?" Deter had a vivid picture of a bionic Iron Man-type robotic limb. She shivered; what world had she just woken up to?

"Well... I can show you if you promise not to freak out."

She nodded.

Lincoln stood up and slowly pulled off his T-shirt.

DETER

She blacked out again, but not before she had taken in the full horror of what she saw. It was a far cry from her innocent existence up on her terrace suite of the Plaza overlooking Central Park. She awoke this morning to the sun streaming in through the two big windows standing nearly floor to ceiling, letting the early-morning sun cast shadows on the serene pale green carpet. There was no shadow of the knowledge that now shattered her dreams.

She liked to wake late, but she must have forgotten to close the curtains last night. Turning her face away from the brightness and hunching up the covers, she realised she managed to end up on the other side of the bed again. She wondered what it would be like to share a bed with somebody. Comforting in many ways, she imagined, but limiting in others; she wasn't sure she'd be good at sharing her space.

She never had to share space with anyone, not even her parents. Deter couldn't remember her parents. No one talked about them to her and as she had no memories of them, she didn't feel their loss. If she had known and loved them, of course she'd feel very differently. Even so, she felt their absence, especially at times like this.

Deter's life ran like clockwork and although she went through a phase of rebelling a couple of years ago, she was not only resigned to but enjoyed being cushioned by the familiarity of her days.

Every weekday was the same. Mr Jameson arrived at 8am and Deter had always made sure she was up and ready before he arrived. When she was younger, Amery used to come and wake her at 7.30, help her wash and dress, and pretty much do all the mum things. When she was thirteen it was decided, probably by Amery, that she could be responsible for waking herself and getting herself up and ready. Deter made sure that she was always up by the time Jameson knocked so she could open the door for him. Mr Jameson belonged to the hotel, well, he worked there and was the butler assigned to Deter to bring her breakfast. He replaced another man when she was about seven, who she remembered as very pale and a bit wobbly. He wasn't old, but he moved cautiously as though he was creeping slowly and uncertainly towards his dotage. Mr Jameson was the opposite – robust, tall and purposeful – but although she saw him every day, he remained rigidly professional in how he addressed her. During her rebellious phase, she used to try and get him to break character by asking personal questions. The only time he'd reacted was when she'd asked him, in a goading and provoking tone, about his family: "Is there a Mrs Jameson? Do tell? Is she very sexy?" She put great emphasis on the 'sexy', aiming more to ridicule than compliment. "Bet she's a real looker."

Mr Jameson, oblivious to the undertones of her questions, looked pleased and nodded. "She is a wonderful woman, I'm very lucky to have her in my life."

"What about little Jamesons? Bet you have lots of children, are they like me?"

Instantly, and shockingly, she realised by Jameson's face that something she said had upset him enormously. He was trying not to show it, but the way he looked so broken made her feel deeply ashamed. He hadn't answered and she hadn't needed him to. She knew something sad and terrible had happened. She was never disrespectful towards him again.

Today was a Saturday, and she slowly got out of bed, wishing the bright sun hadn't woken her so early; she began what felt like the long walk downstairs to the bathroom. She looked at everything as she passed it carefully, unconsciously making photos in her head so that every inch of her childhood home would be recorded. Did she know somehow that this was the day her life would change? She noted the way the walls looked a different colour on the staircase, even though Amery swore it was the trick of the light. The little secret messages from years ago that you could only see if you peeled the stair carpet back from the skirting: 'I will never wear a dress' and 'pink sucks', defiant scrawlings to mark her determination to be a tomboy. She smiled, enjoying the memories and feeling a warm rush of love for Amery, who was such a wonderful part of her life.

Outside, far below, too small for her to see clearly, the city picked up its pace. Traffic was starting to build up and the sun already heating up the pavement. Across the city was Asher, the boy she had met at the Metropolitan Museum a few weeks ago. Asher had been so friendly, grateful even to meet her, as though he was starved of contact with other young people. *Maybe*, she thought, *he's of a similar social standing to me or Amery would never have let us continue chatting*. He'd been so kind when some rough people had tried to take her handbag. Both he and the security guards had run after them. She couldn't wait to see him again... not that she fancied him, oh no, nothing like that, but he did have lovely eyes. Especially when he smiled at her.

After she washed and dressed, she flumped down on the small, rather formal, two-seater sofa. She decided to while away the time until breakfast by turning on the television and sitting in a sort of mesmerised trance watching children's cartoons. It wasn't until she heard a firm knock on the door that she realised that half an hour had just slid past, albeit accompanied by unrealistically high-pitched voices and glorious technicolour. Quickly turning it off, she leapt up to let Jameson in. He looked even more resolutely bland and serene this morning, and after laying out her breakfast things he stepped back and waited for her to dismiss him. As she ate her three-minute eggs, she kept him standing there, hoping to engage him in conversation, but it was all business as usual.

"Anything else I can get you, Miss D?"

"No, Jameson, thank you, I have everything."

After Jameson left, Deter slowly finished eating and felt tempted to put the television back on, but thought better of it, in case Amery arrived early.

This morning they planned to meet Deter's friends Jenny and Padma at their favourite coffee shop. They usually hung out a bit then went shopping and Deter was looking forward to seeing them; Luigi's had the very best coffee and delicious homemade pastries!

When Deter was little, Amery had been very soft and cuddly, and as she had grown up, Amery's role had also changed. Now taking on the responsibilities of life coach, headmistress, event planner and bodyguard, Amery went everywhere with her. Deter didn't mind, as she totally understood and respected her guardian's position.

AMERY

Amery was late that morning as she hurried along the corridor. The professor from the Establishment was just behind her; she could hear his short legs trying to keep up. The corridor was covered in a luxurious, thick pile carpet, which made walking in heels much harder work and even though Deter's rooms were just off the lift, the brief walk somehow seemed to be taking ages. In their quick meeting downstairs, she'd found the way the doctor talked about Deter rather rude and she hoped he was going to be a little politer to her in person. He wasn't Deter's usual doctor. Professor Joseph came from the top and he had a snide way of smiling at everything Amery said as though he knew more than her, about everything. It was most irritating! He spoke about Deter as though he knew everything about her, despite not having met her yet.

Amery paused at the door, allowing the professor to catch up, and so she could calm her thoughts. Deter wasn't expecting a visitor.

"Come in," Deter called out, after hearing Amery's knock on the door.

"Deter, this is Professor Joseph. He's the head of the practice that's always looked after your family, and now you're nearly eighteen he would like to invite you to his clinic for a full scan and assessment. I know Doctor Phillips always examined you here, but slightly more rigorous tests are needed for insurance purposes. The policy changes once you become an adult."

"Yes, of course." Deter knew how body scanning was important. As she was the sole heir of the Edison fortune, she was treated like a precious jewel. Buffed, polished, viewed through special lenses, prodded, poked and measured. It wasn't a big deal.

"A few questions, here, now in the comfort of your own home, then later, at approximately 3pm this afternoon, Miss Nix will escort you to my clinic for full body tests. You will be staying with us a while."

Staying? No one had mentioned that before. Deter shot an intensely worried gaze at Amery, but still she had not responded. What about her friends? They were expecting to meet her this morning.

"Stand for me, look ahead and keep still."

Amery sensed that Deter was looking to her for reassurance, as the professor's manner was a little abrupt. Amery didn't meet her eye. She wanted Deter to know that she didn't like the professor or his plans either, but it was important to be accommodating.

"Now tell me. Any abscesses, open wounds?"

"No."

"Any redness or unusual swelling?"

"No."

"Fever or chills?"

"No, I'm perfectly well."

"Blisters, black scabs?"

"Urgh! No."

"Good." He smiled. "I need some blood if that's OK? I can make a start on tests straight away when I get back. I have a couple more meetings here in New York first, but I'm looking forward to our further sessions."

Deter looked at Amery and raised her eyebrows.

The doctor bent to retrieve his equipment from his bag. "Do I have your permission?" The professor indicated towards the needle and small vials he laid out in front of them.

Amery finally looked at her and rolled her eyes conspiratorially. Deter nodded, smiled and rolled up her sleeves. As she had held her arm out, the doctor pushed her sleeves further up her arm, looking satisfied and almost delighted that he was about to draw her blood. Amery wasn't surprised he was excited; it was the first Immune arm he had seen for a while. She sighed and looked away. She couldn't bear seeing the moment the needle pierced the skin. The professor seemed to be loving it!

LINCOLN

Oh dear, that hadn't gone well. Show a girl your chest and she passes out!

That morning, in anticipation of her arrival, he laid out small syringes, blood collection tubes, a tourniquet and some cotton balls. Everything they needed to know could be learnt from a few blood samples.

He stopped to collect his breath as he looked at the collection of instruments and then double-checked his schedule. He pushed his sleeves up, although they were already rolled up high; it was a reflexive habit, as he couldn't bear the feel of fabric restricting his arms. When he was getting keyed up about something, it was something he did repeatedly.

"Hey, I'm talking to you, Lincoln!"

He turned round quickly to see Hugo glaring angrily at him.

"Sorry, Hugo, I was busy making sure I hadn't missed out any of your instructions."

"We won't get this chance again, not in a long time, so just make sure you don't make a single error."

"You can count on me, you know that."

"Yeah." Hugo ran his fingers through his hair, starting to calm down, although he still had a frown. "This is the chance we've been waiting for, so the Establishment will start taking us seriously."

"No violence, though, I don't want the Immune damaged. It could have very negative repercussions all round." Lincoln tried to sound as firm as he dared with Hugo.

"Agreed, everyone knows that if we step over the line from being a pressure group to taking a forceful stance, then we'll be in more trouble than we could handle."

'Tell that to Angus!"

"Angus has been reined in. He knows the stakes are high."

Hugo moved over to the bed that was prepared for the Immune and touched the sheets. "Pink sheets? This isn't a pyjama party! Just remember she'll be our hostage and as her main keeper, the last thing we want is for her to form an attachment to you."

"Doesn't matter if she does. It won't be reciprocated," Lincoln replied quickly.

The idea of an Immune filled Lincoln with a mixture of fear, jealousy and, unfortunately, admiration. They were so rare, with rock-star quality, and this one was also a world away, so wealthy, isolated and spoilt, the very idea of her annoyed him. She could afford the best treatment, the best prosthetics and new organs, and she didn't even need them. They had been observing her for a while and they were pretty confident that she would be at Luigi's on Saturday morning. They had very nearly been successful in capturing her at the Metropolitan Museum two weeks ago, but they had been intercepted by security. They were determined not to fail this time.

Feeling nervous, he busied himself with rearranging the equipment in size order.

"How long will it take to test her blood?" Hugo watched him impatiently. "We want to confirm to the world that a Complete Immune is in our possession."

"Oh, it will be pretty quick. I will know by tomorrow morning."

"Excellent, then we can push on to Stage 2 tomorrow."

"I've already told you that's impossible. I want to carry out full MRI and ultrasound scans. The only time I can do that is when Nathan's on duty in the hospital. He said he's not in until next Wednesday."

"Lincoln, waiting that long will be such a gamble. We'd be giving them five days in which to find her."

"We agreed I could carry out the tests! Using the genes of a Complete is all very well, but what if we discover that she carries other genetic traits? Look at the horror the cure has caused."

"No, you're right, if she's to be the basis of our future gene pool, she must be absolutely clean."

"Right, then Stage 2 will just have to wait."

Hugo sighed loudly. "Agreed."

Lincoln joined the Faction when he was still at medical school. He wanted to be a doctor to help combat the effects of FED. He had known about FED all his life. His parents both had it, neither of them particularly severely, and for a while it looked as though he wasn't going to be affected, but after being struck low with an ordinary bout of flu he developed a terrible fever overnight and by morning black swellings appeared all over his body. These then turned into huge, painful blisters, which instead of healing crusted over then flaked off, taking massive chunks of suppurating flesh with them. Because it was so severe, he was rushed to hospital, where it became clear he would need both arms amputated and a new chest cavity. His organs were undamaged, but his heart had been affected somehow and was under supervision. It was thought to be a form of myocarditis caused by his immune system getting confused and attacking his heart. He was being constantly monitored and they fitted him with a clear plastic chest covering so that his heart could be observed without intrusive surgery.

He was on the list for a new heart, but the system tended to favour those who could pay the highest price. If there had only been a vaccine, he would still be Complete, someone who is not Immune but by luck or owing to the cure, they have no limb loss. Being Complete was considered highly desirable amongst the elite and they spent thousands of pounds on disguising their disabilities and paying for realistic prosthetics. This was the opposite of the less privileged who, if they didn't have bright and obvious new limbs, were happy to have their disabilities on display.

His medical background made him highly valuable to the Faction and he passionately believed that the Establishment had made misguided decisions in trying to combat FED. FED was a particularly virulent strain of Flesh-Eating Disease that hit globally eighty years ago and slowly decimated the population. Remote, isolated populations were the first to be affected, followed by less privileged communities, until only the wealthiest cities remained. Small, infected villages and towns declared themselves quarantined, but it didn't stop the spread. If FED didn't kill you, then an associated infection would. Only the strongest survived. Nearly sixty years it took to find an effective cure, but the cure came with a price. Not only was it prohibitively expensive, but the new generation of children, although disease-free, were born with hideous defects. Deformities so monstrous and painful that euthanasia at birth was the kindest option. The human race was diseased and dying out.

The Establishment had one hope and that was to experiment with embryos that came from naturally immune parents. The number of Immunes was low and they tended to be found in isolated pockets in wealthy communities. Although she didn't know it yet, one of these Immunes was Deter.

But while the Establishment was focussing time and money on breeding the disease out, the Faction wanted a quicker solution. They wanted Deter so that they could analyse her blood to help create a vaccine. Surely this was the most logical and effective solution?

DETER

Deter watched Amery carefully as they travelled twenty floors down in the lift, but Amery wasn't giving anything away. Today was not a usual day. Tests with the weirdo doctor had just been the start. Now they were rushing across the state to a vast clinic over five hours away. Amery seemed flinchy and more anxious about security than usual. And now they were late.

"Late for what? It's only a few tests," she asked.

"It doesn't do to keep everyone waiting," Amery replied.

"And why did we have to pack so much?"

"You never know."

"Well, you obviously do, but just aren't telling me," Deter huffed.

Deter hated it when Amery fussed. She also hated it when Amery didn't tell her everything. She always knew when Amery was holding information back and it really riled her. She was nearly eighteen and she vowed that once she became an adult and in charge of her own affairs this entire cloak and dagger nonsense would stop. She realised she was starting to feel increasingly angry, becoming hot with irritation, and hoped that Amery wouldn't notice. To control herself, she dug her fingernails hard into her wrist.

Amery pursed her lips and continued, "You know how precious you are to me. I know you're cross with me, but it is my job is to protect you." She reached out and put her arm around the girl's shoulders, squeezing all the affection she felt for her into her small frame.

"Come here."

Instantly, Deter burst into tears. "It's just, well, I'm not unhappy, as obviously I trust that you know what's best, but how long am I to stay at the clinic? Can my friends visit?"

"I'm sure they can. Come on, let's make our way to the car."

Deter hesitated and stood anxiously as Amery held out her hand and then pulled her across the foyer. Jameson came to say goodbye, and she impulsively hugged him tight. For once he stooped and clasped her back, and she felt hot tears returning.

"I'm going to really miss you, Jameson."

"I'm sure it won't be long. I bought you this." He held out a tiny, beautifully wrapped parcel and said, "Open it later."

"Thank you so much, thank you," she cried, now openly sobbing; she fumbled trying to put it in her bag but couldn't find the opening through her tears, so she slipped it into her pocket.

Sitting in the car, she felt her anxiety rise to her throat, tightening her chest and making it hard to swallow. Behind her had been the usual security vehicle and she knew that there was another one somewhere either in front or alongside. It had always been like that, one of the necessary but at times irritating side effects of being extremely wealthy. Amery had impressed on her from a young age that she was a potential kidnapping target and that everyone she saw was vetted and chaperoned. Jenny and Padma understood, as they were in exactly the same position. If only she could see them, they could be sitting in the last of the summer sun, flirting with the waiters at Luigi's. A five-hour journey might be possible for special occasions, but gone would be the days of casual Sunday brunches and studying together. She was aware that Amery was busy directing the driver as it looked like traffic was building up coming out of the city and they hadn't even made it over the river yet. The driver made a detour, turning off through a side street.

"I knew we should have left earlier," Amery fretted. "Look, we're pretty much stuck where we started, and our exit is miles ahead. Let's see if we can jump the traffic."

Gazing across the street, pretending to be concerned, Deter realised they were now going right past Luigi's. Her mood lifted as she spotted two familiar faces. "Amery, look! It's Jenny and Padma! They've seen me! Jenny, Padma!" She simultaneously waved and tugged at Amery's sleeve. "Oh please, can we stop? I can say a proper goodbye!"

"There isn't time!"

"But the traffic isn't going anywhere, please, just for a few minutes to say goodbye."

"Oh, very well, driver, please unlock the door." Amery looked apprehensive and checked her watch. She looked out the window to ensure that the security guards who were following had seen they were exiting the vehicle and made a quick signal with her hand to indicate she wanted them to follow.

Deter rushed forward, calling out excitedly, but then just as she reached them, something tripped her up. She fell hard on the pavement and as she tried to get up, she looked up at her friends to try to reassure them but was shocked to see two men violently assaulting them. People say that when traumatic things happen it's almost as if they play out in front of you in slow motion. Deter had never believed that, until now. She felt so powerless. Her body couldn't move fast enough; she was too far away. Padma was shouting and screaming as a man held back her arms and forced her to the ground. Jenny was already restrained and Deter could see the gag over her mouth was so tight her face was distorted, and tears soaked into the grubby fabric. Angry, she lunged forward, only for her shoulder to be jerked back as she was grabbed and held back. The last thing she was aware of was Amery screaming her name as Deter felt something pulled over her head and pressure applied to her neck before she passed out.

AMERY

In the melee that followed, Amery panicked for the first time. Never in the nearly eighteen years of looking after Deter had things been out of her control, until now.

There had been some pretty worrying situations. Once when Deter was small she had been watching the television when an advert for a new prosthesis came on.

> *Do you want life-like skin that sweats in the heat and has goosebumps in the cold?*
>
> *Thanks to incredible new research, we now have new limbs just for you. They link to your own sensory nerves so that touch and temperature can be experienced authentically.*
>
> *Build a new life and new body with us, one that has hi-spec sensors to combat phantom pain and is truly all you.*

Deter was fascinated and Amery had quickly turned it off and reported to the Establishment that keeping her apart from general society was going to cause problems. She argued that Deter would be quite able to accept that she was different and that keeping her ignorant was going to cause issues at some point. The Establishment didn't agree. They decided that all television programmes in Deter's rooms would be under their control and not contain any information or references to FED. They knew that previous Immune specimens reacted badly to being so valued and that breeding programmes were much more successful if they could live stress-free and in ignorance of the infected. It was best if they knew nothing of their origins and that they were brought up in a carefully protected environment enjoying the best education and luxury. Amery knew nothing of Deter's true heritage but accepted the story that had been created and continued to carry out her duties with diligence and genuine care.

The only other threat had come recently, when the Faction tried to seize Deter at the Metropolitan Museum. Amery saw three men circling around and acting suspiciously. She immediately alerted Deter's bodyguards, who snapped into action, rendering two out of the three useless; the third lunged at Deter, but without the backup of his friends, he had no hope. Security chased him off. Luckily, Deter hadn't realised how serious it could have been and was excited by the drama and the role Asher played in it. She seemed to think the men had been after her handbag, and Amery was happy to let her.

Also unknown to Deter was that underneath her own clothes Amery had terrible scars from when the disease affected her in her childhood. It had eaten her away, from her feet upwards. All the bones in her legs up to her pelvic girdle were replaced with metal and plastic prosthetics. Even her lower organs, colon, kidneys and liver were not her own.

She had chosen realistic designs, perfectly matching her flesh colour and being a child at the time, adapted incredibly quickly to her new body. She had heard that young people from the less well-off communities had a fashion for brightly coloured prosthetics and even see-through ones. Like most wealthy Americans, Amery couldn't understand why anyone would want to draw attention to their disease-ravaged bodies.

Amery tried to control her breathing but felt weak and disorientated. Padma, Jenny and Deter had disappeared, and the traffic was in chaos. Drivers and passengers who had witnessed the assault were either out of their cars, trying to make sense of what happened, or keeping their heads down and eyes averted, avoiding involvement. Security for the girls were conferring and orchestrating retrieval, but the attack had been so fast and unexpected that no one had much to go on. Who would believe that three Immunes, the only three in America, kept hidden in this vast city for nearly eighteen years, would all go missing on the same day at the same time in the same place? No one could have known they'd all be here on the corner of 2nd Avenue at 11.30am outside a boutique coffee shop.

All these years Amery had been preparing Deter for such an attack, but talking about it in theory was one thing, actually living through the reality of it was another. Plus, Deter would assume it was owing to her wealth that she was being held to ransom. She had no idea of her true value to the human race.

Amery took a deep breath and steeled herself as she prepared to call the Establishment.

DETER

The first time she regained consciousness Deter became aware of a terrible smell. It hit the back of her throat and spread a noxious pain up through her body. The pain outweighed her rising panic and could have taken over if she hadn't felt weighed down with raw and violent bruising. She moaned softly as she tried to move. Cautiously, she opened her eyes but couldn't see. Disoriented, she blinked and for a moment was anxious that she lost her sight until she realised she was in a dark room. Her head was pounding and she tried to work out if she was alone, her breathing and her heart too loud. She knew it was vital to try and calm herself down; someone could hear her, be waiting to overpower her again. Paralysed with fear, she laid there, focussing on slowing her breath and trying to give her eyes a chance to get used to the lack of light.

Deter stayed there for what felt like hours, sweat pouring from her body, until she was sure there was no one else in the room. The same thoughts ran around her head. *Who had done this? Why? And where am I?* She hoped that Jenny and Padma were somewhere safe and that their bodyguards had managed to protect them. Her own team would be distraught; Amery desperate to find her. She whimpered gently, the agony of being separated from her guardian more painful than her aching body. Cautiously she felt around and patted the soft surface beneath her. It felt like a bed. She fumbled around for the edge, then gingerly sat up and slowly swung her legs off the edge. Suddenly feeling nauseous, she sat very still as she waited for the hot, clammy feeling that accompanied it to fade. Cautiously, she steadied herself she stood up slowly, just as a bright light flooded the room. Temporarily blinded and completely shocked by the extreme change, she threw up and collapsed to the ground.

LINCOLN

Lincoln hadn't prepared for three of them. He also wasn't prepared for them having been so violently restrained. It upset him and made him feel uneasy about looking after them. There were painful swellings on Deter's neck and shoulders, and Padma couldn't move her arms, as the bruising was so severe. Jenny had cuts to her knees where she had fallen and her face was swollen from the gag that Angus had tied so tightly. When Hugo had called him in a state of high excitement, it had taken a minute or two to work out what was going on.

"What are you saying? Do you have her or not?" Lincoln was confused.

"Aren't you listening? We have three of them!"

"How do you know they are all Immunes?"

"That's just it!" Hugo's pitch was rising. "Talk about an unexpected twist of fate!"

"I don't understand," Lincoln said, "what are you doing with three of them? Where are we going to put them?"

"That's your problem! I'm bringing them in now!"

"Where am I supposed to put them?"

"You'll work out something. Man! You should've seen Angus's face when we realised what we had! We thought two of them were just troublemakers. Angus was teaching them a thing or two when something about them just didn't seem right, you know? Can't even put my finger on it. Must be an in-built Immune sensor."

Lincoln frowned. "What's the plan for them? Where are we going to keep them? Am I testing all three?"

"Jesus, Lincoln, you're such a killjoy. We'll be with you in ten!"

Feeling wrong-footed, Lincoln made his way to the room he'd prepared for Deter. He knew all about her. He knew she was eighteen in six days' time. She was small, five foot two inches with dark, straight hair. She studied hard, was privileged, sheltered and completely naïve to the real world. He knew all this from hacking into the Establishment's databases. He'd been preparing for her arrival for weeks. He had no idea who the other two were. Males? Females? Age? Physical details? Interests? Habits? It was going to be such a stretch to the budget as well. He coughed and pushed up his sleeves, as he thought carefully about how he could best utilise space and resources.

AMERY

Amery felt enormously betrayed and angry. Professor Joseph was still talking, but she had stopped listening. Around her was her security team and also Padma's and Jenny's parents. She had completely believed that Padma and Jenny were Immunes, but although they weren't Immune, they were Complete. So wealthy, their families had paid a vast sum at the first sign of slight blistering to cure their daughters of FED. They had no scars and, also like Deter, no idea of the true horror of the disease. This meant they probably had no idea that they would never be able to have healthy children. For some reason the Establishment had decided they made ideal companions for Deter and orchestrated their friendship. Why she wasn't trusted with this information she didn't know, but it made her suspect that the Establishment had a secret agenda and that made her incredibly angry. Worse than that, she felt used and manipulated.

Jenny's mother had been sobbing for the past half an hour and both sets of parents looked absolutely distraught. *What a bloody mess we live in,* thought Amery. The professor had handed over to the head of security, a surprisingly small but forceful man, who was trying to salvage the situation. He offered the parents practical advice and explained how his team was working on tracking the girls down. With a combination of old-fashioned detective work, state-of-the-art surveillance, coupled with sniffer dogs and drone spyware, he had faith they would find them soon.

Everyone in regular contact with Deter was being treated suspiciously, even Amery. She was asked to remain at the Establishment in allocated rooms and she soon learnt that all tutors and Jameson had also been detained. Every inch of the apartment and all of Deter's belongings were being examined. Was it possible that Deter had not gone unwillingly? Could the girls be working for the Faction? Amery knew this was utter rubbish but had to let security do their job.

Alone in her room, she lay down and tried to sleep. Tears pricked as images of Deter flitted through her mind like a slideshow. Deter as a baby, gazing up at her trustingly when Amery first held her in her arms. Deter running, completely over-excited, across the beach in a rare trip to the coast. Deter's little arms clasped tight around her neck at bedtime, sobbing, "Don't leave me!" Deter, hot and pink in a mood over wardrobe disagreements. Amery's heart flooded with love at the memories; they had a connection that ran powerfully deep and remained constant. She was her baby, her child and her responsibility. How could she let her be taken away?

Feeling useless and frustrated by her imprisonment, Amery sat back up and gave herself a talking to. She needed information. She needed to find out what exactly the Establishment was planning. What if Deter couldn't be found, or something terrible had happened to all the girls? She also needed to know how long Deter had been expected to stay at the clinic, and what about afterwards? She had been told they were relocating to Italy, but she didn't trust anything the Establishment said now. She resolved to find out as much as she could and would start by having a little chat with Professor Joseph.

LINCOLN

Lincoln was worried. He had to break the news to Angus and Hugo that the two girls Padma and Jenny were not Immunes after all. Scarring on their feet showed that they had FED in the past, and their blood confirmed that the virus was held in check by large doses of the cure. This would pop their balloon of big ideas. Angus would be particularly angry. Last night they had held a riotous and celebratory meeting, toasting their good luck and replanning their strategy.

"We must send the Establishment a warning. Let them know we hold their prize possessions. Tell them we'll go public with this and when the people hear that they've been hothousing a superior race, they'll be absolutely destroyed," Angus crowed.

"Why warn them, why not just go public?" Hugo was impatient.

"Because at the moment the Establishment don't know for certain that it's us who has them; they suspect, but they can't prove it."

Angus couldn't sit still he was so excited. It was unusual for his and Hugo's roles to be reversed, but he was a more cunning strategic planner than most people suspected.

"We currently hold the biggest card in our hands, so we mustn't over-play it!"

One of the new members Lincoln didn't recognise pushed forward, eagerly looking at Angus for approval.

"Right. I'd like to suggest we drip feed the public pictures and statements. Such as, 'the Complete myth... or is it?' maybe accompanied by a photo of Deter but black out her face?"

Angus nodded in agreement. "Yes! We must stress our position by using words like, 'elite', 'super race', 'secret', 'breeding programme', 'conspiracy'. If we drip feed it on social media, it'll soon spread like wildfire."

There was a buzz of excitement.

"Errr... I have some practical issues I'd like to discuss." Lincoln hesitated as everyone turned to face him. He nearly lost his nerve as he saw Hugo frowning at him, but he took a deep breath and ploughed on. "We have funding and room prepared for one captive but not three. What am I expected to feed them, and will I be given help guarding them? Where am I supposed to put them? At the moment Deter is locked in the room prepared for her, but the other two are currently in my room. We need rotas and I need help."

There was a pause and then someone childishly sniggered, "You need help, all right!"

Angus rolled his eyes. "OK. This is something we need to address. Hugo, is there enough money to feed three of them and for how long? Maybe there's someone here willing to sponsor them?"

One of the newer recruits stepped forward eagerly. "I know my family would be keen to support this if they knew the full story. So I'll definitely be able to provide food and I'd happily help on a rota too."

"Excellent, thank you, James." Angus looked round for further volunteers, but nothing was forthcoming. "Oh, come on, I know it's not exciting or glamorous, but we need more than two of you."

"I don't want to touch them," said a spotty boy at the back.

"No, me neither, they're freaks," said another.

"I know how you feel, but they are just like us really." Lincoln sighed, as Angus glared at everyone.

"If no one volunteers, it's simple. I'll assign soldiers myself and oversee the rota personally. However, volunteers would be highly appreciated."

Everyone shifted uncomfortably and several reluctant hands went up. Lincoln was amazed that Angus was supporting him. Angus was surprising everyone this evening.

Sleeping arrangements were shifted, a couple of people volunteered to bunk down together and by the end of the evening each Complete was locked into their own room, with a guard on duty outside. Lincoln's status went up and by following Angus's lead, everyone became a little more deferential. After all, as Angus pointed out, the success of the vaccine relied totally on Lincoln's skill. So he might be a boring, geeky prat, but he was their boring, geeky prat, and they should show some respect.

Now, he was clutching the results of the immunity tests as he knocked apprehensively on Angus's room door.

"Enter!" Angus called out. "And…?" he added eagerly when he saw Lincoln was clutching some paperwork.

"Umm… I'm afraid we have only one Immune. The original target Deter has natural immunity. Both the others have standard resistance owing to past infection of FED, but not enough for our purposes. They are no different to you or me. Just lucky, as they were administered the cure at very early stages. There's no obvious visible damage, just minimal scarring. Very easy to mistake them for Immunes."

"Does anyone else know this?"

"Not yet, just you and me."

"Let's keep it that way, for now."

"It's so disappointing, as having three different genetic sources would have been so valuable to our research."

"I'm sure the girls will have their uses." Angus clenched his frustration tightly in his fist. He didn't want Lincoln to know how much this news had affected him.

Lincoln nodded and quickly made his way back to his room. Whatever Angus was planning he didn't want to know.

ANGUS

Once the door closed, Angus slammed his hand down hard on his desk, shattering the worktop and causing the wrist of his prosthesis to bend at an awkward angle. He ripped his now-useless arm off and threw it at the door.

He knew it had been too good to be true. Three Immunes wouldn't just fall into his hands so easily. Still, the girls could be useful to fuel negative propaganda, even if they couldn't be used for vaccine research. He just needed a way to hype up the public so that the Faction could push the Establishment a little bit further. He was itching to take the campaign up a notch. Enough of all this peaceful pressurising; it hadn't got them anywhere.

He opened his wardrobe door. Alongside his jeans and T-shirts was a sealed unit, which was temperature-controlled to store his collection of extreme prosthetics. All custom-made, they were far from natural-looking, unlike the cast-off limb that now lay on his bedroom floor. There was a sleek, dark blue arm with tiny, silver stars that could fire ten small grenades, with built-in lasers to intercept any incoming grenades. The grenades could be pre-programmed and could be a mix of lethal and non-lethal. He currently had six fragmentation grenades to cause as much damage as possible, but also one smoke grenade, one fire grenade, plus two illuminating ones, to cover all eventualities on the field. Angus had been training hard for years and now felt ready to use them.

A second prosthesis, slightly longer than his arm would be if it were still intact, housed a rapid-fire gun charged by electricity and emergency solar with ten hours' combat time. No recoil, no sound, no heat, it was an efficient and undercover instrument of death. It glowed angrily in a hot orangey-red to show it was fully charged and ready for action. He switched the colour to dark green and checked it was loaded. No good for long forays but perfect for quick recces.

The last had no weapons loaded on it but was linked to his helmet and body armour. With it he could control colour and thermo qualities to stay camouflaged and comfortable in any temperature. It wasn't fancy, but it was lightweight and housed all the chips to monitor his physical well-being: heart rate, body temperature and energy levels. It also housed a monitor to measure the proximity to both his own men and nearby enemy troops.

Kneeling, eyes tight shut, as though in front of a holy shrine, he offered a fervent prayer: "Lord, make me to know mine end, and the measure of my days, what it is; that I may know how frail I am." He knew that what would be, would be, and trusting in Him, he set his disappointment aside.

Rising with hope and purpose, he slung all three limbs over his shoulder using a special harness and practised rapidly removing one arm and attaching another. He felt ready.

MARIA

Maria was tired. She closed the fridge door but not until it had startled her by beeping a warning signal. Standing too long with it open, hopelessly wishing there was more in it, she resolved that things were going to change.

Firstly, she was going to smile and cook the most amazing supper with one egg, a couple of cold cauliflower florets and a dried-up crust of cheese. With a dash of milk to make a sauce, it would be just enough for Selina. She would do without food tonight, as she would have a snack at work tomorrow. There were always biscuits in the staff canteen. If she took her break slightly late, she might be able to steal a couple extra if she was lucky. Selina loved them too.

Maria hobbled over to the cooker and began melting butter ready to add the flour to make a roux. Her stump was sore after another day on her feet, cleaning at the school. She would have loved to upgrade her prosthetics, but all her money had gone to look after Selina. She tucked her long, dark curls behind her ears and sighed as she thought of Selina's father. He left Maria absolutely broke and broken as he'd moved on to a new life and new wife. *Bastard!* Maria had to remind herself every day that nothing mattered anymore except Selina. They still had her mother's flat and just enough food and Selina was still one hundred per cent healthy. She kept her at home to avoid infection and keep her safe from the outside world's many dangers.

"Shall we play Monopoly tonight?" Selina loved all the old-fashioned games. Ian had been so competitive and they had spent many happy hours together playing; Scrabble, chess and dominoes were her favourites. Even now Selina would play solitaire and pairs to while away the lonely hours.

Maria was so tired, but she smiled as she put the tiny dish of cauliflower cheese in the oven. "Only if I can be the little dog."

"Of course you can, Mummy, I want to be the top hat today."

They had an antique set of die cast tokens, over one hundred years old and her mother's pride and joy. There used to be a ship, but it had gone missing a few years ago and Maria had turned the flat upside down looking for it. They would be worth quite a bit, but Maria wouldn't dream of selling them. Every link to the happy times they'd had as a family was unbelievably precious. Sometimes Selina insisted on playing for Ian and another piece would be laid out for him. It made Maria's chest feel tight with the weight of her grief, but she could see how much comfort Selina derived from this occasional ritual, so she would smile and go along with it.

Adjusting to being without Ian brought miserable challenges. Being a single mum was such a lonely path to walk with no support or guidance. Was she doing the right thing, taking Selina out of school? How could she afford the bills that arrived with what seemed like increasing regularity? All the big questions and the small ones too that she had to answer herself every day. Then there was the anger: anger, jealousy and deep resentment. It was so unfair, she had no one to hold or comfort her, whereas Ian's new wife had everything.

They had only just laid out the game when Maria remembered Selina's supper was still in the oven. It was bubbly and smelt unbelievably good for something so simple.

"Oh, yum!" Selina got the plates out.

"It's OK, I've already eaten, this is all yours." Selina put one of the plates back. Maria cut off a small slice of bread. "Here, better eat it before we get too stuck into the game."

"This was Daddy's favourite!" said Selina happily as she scooped some sauce up with her bread.

"Was it? I thought he liked sweet and sour chicken."

"Oh, yes, that was his favourite too, but he liked scraping the slightly burnt bits of sauce from the dish. He said it was the best thing ever."

Maria watched Selina eating. She had Ian's mouth and her nose. There were so many little unique things too that didn't seem to come from either of them; she was so perfect. Looking at her, Maria's heart felt so full, it sustained her through the toughest times.

The game went on for several hours, during which time Maria managed to acquire the utilities, but ended up having to sell her hotels as Selina owned pretty much all the top streets. If only you were rewarded in real life for going around in circles, and imagine what you could do with a get out of jail card!

By 10pm, Maria was ready for bed, but Selina seemed to have found her second wind. Listening to her chatting continuously while washing and undressing, Maria smiled at her daughter, nodded and then eventually clasped Selina in one long, hard embrace, squeezing her so tight and peppering her long, dark hair with kisses. There's nothing in the world she wouldn't do to keep her precious girl safe.

DETER

Deter looked at her hands and arms carefully. She had a very small mole on her left wrist and a scar on her chin from when she tripped up the stairs as a child. The only other blemishes were from the recent attack. Grazes on her knees and elbows, and a bruise around her neck.

How could this be an anomaly?

She still couldn't get over seeing Lincoln's chest. It was a clear, plastic cage and his heart was a dark purple. It was disgusting but also compulsive viewing. Like a goldfish tank, it had a hypnotic, mesmerising effect as the heart beat rhythmically. Somehow, the worst thing was finding out his hands and arms weren't real. The texture was pretty realistic and the movement perfect, no clunkiness or awkwardness at all.

She felt as if she'd fallen into a dream world and was now finding out that this nightmare was reality. Nothing Amery taught her had prepared her for this. Was she the only one who didn't have a disease-ravaged body? What of Jenny and

Padma? Where were they and did they know about FED and if so, were they hiding plastic limbs under their designer clothes? Her mind was bursting with questions.

There was very little to do except sit and think and wait for Lincoln's next visit. At first, she'd tried to monitor outside movement and look for opportunities to escape. But it soon became clear that the Faction was made up of highly competent soldiers and that she had no hope of finding her way out. Every now and then she heard voices outside and at first she tried to yell for attention, but they either couldn't hear her or they were ignoring her. She often found herself sobbing, which was so unlike her, for she never cried, but it was more out of frustration and confusion than sadness.

There was a click as the lock turned, so Deter rubbed her eyes and sat up.

"I've come to ask for your help." Lincoln set a screen up on the table next to her. It was the only table and he struggled to move it nearer so they could both sit on the bed and look at it together. She was pleased to see him but didn't want him to know it.

"The Faction want answers about you and your friends. So we're going to see what we can find on the Establishment's database."

"What if I refuse to help?" she retorted. "And where are my friends?"

"Your friends are safe and will remain so, as long as you co-operate."

"Oh my God, they are here too? Why can't I see them?"

"You can once we know more about you all," Lincoln said cautiously.

Deter was so relieved to hear that Jenny and Padma were all right. She had hoped their own security guards had saved them, but she was pleased to hear she wasn't alone.

"I'm not sure I want to know any more. What you've told me so far has been quite unpleasant."

"Well, let's just say that if you don't help me, we'll both be in trouble, and anyway, I thought you wanted answers yourself." Lincoln began typing.

"I do," Deter sighed, "but I don't see why I should help you." She sighed again dramatically.

He smiled and, shrugging, turned the screen so only he could see it. "Your choice! I'll just keep what I find out to myself." He continued typing and peered at the results that came up in front of him. "Good lord!" He laughed. "I had no idea you were a jigsaw puzzle enthusiast!"

"What?!" She jolted the screen around, but there was just a huge amount of data that made no sense whatever.

"Ha ha! Made you look! OK, let's see if it gives us any info on Jenny. What's her surname?"

"Poppe, that's with two 'P's and an 'E'."

They carried out several dead-end searches on both Jenny and Padma.

"OK, so neither of them feature on the Establishment's records, so that tells us nothing."

"Or maybe it tells us that they are not important enough to monitor. We thought that their connection to you was of relevance to their plans. Maybe they are simply two ordinary but exceptionally wealthy girls who are nothing more than your friends?"

"Is it really that unusual to be so 'complete'? You know, without any evidence of FED?"

"Exceedingly. Everyone has scars. No one has managed to keep all their limbs."

Increasingly curious, she couldn't help asking, "But how come I never knew? What about Amery? I've known her all my life, I would have seen something to give it away, surely?"

"Not if she was careful. Let's have a look at her file."

Deter waited impatiently while Lincoln resumed his search on the computer. Lincoln scanned the results quickly before triumphantly showing Deter.

Deter couldn't believe it. "Almost everything from her waist down is reconstructed!" It didn't seem possible.

"It's pretty standard and don't forget, we've been living like this for years. Don't look so shocked!" Lincoln said.

"But I am! That's just horrific! Everything I've known is being questioned. It also says here that I'm listed as her next of kin. Aren't any of her family on her records?" Frowning, Deter peered at the monitor, looking for more information.

"Nope, nothing."

"But she must have gone home to someone, she used to say, 'I can't stay here all day, some of us have a family to look after, you know!'"

"Didn't you ever ask her?" Lincoln said.

"I must have, but she was good at deflecting questions and I must have been so self-absorbed. I didn't really think of her life beyond her relationship to me. God that makes me feel awful." Deter visibly drooped, eaten up with remorse.

Lincoln wasn't quite sure what to say. This privileged and spoilt girl was having the worst wake-up call. He couldn't help but feel sorry for her.

"Let's see what they say about you." He typed a new code into the system and then added her name.

"Wait! Is there a Jameson mentioned? He worked at the Plaza but was my personal butler," Deter said. Lincoln raised an eyebrow. Deter continued, "I know, I sound like a pampered princess, but I just want to know if he worked for the Establishment too or if he was just a butler."

Lincoln carried out the search as requested and then turned the screen so Deter could see more easily. "It looks like he's 'just' a butler. He's always been in service, starting off as a scullery boy and working his way up. He married quite a wealthy, successful woman. Look at her! Stunning!"

"Yes, he was totally in love with her, and spoke about her with pure joy in his eyes." Deter felt tears gathering as her memories pricked at her conscience.

"Oh!" Lincoln leant forwards, squinting at the screen. "It says they had two children, both deceased."

"No! Really? What happened?" Deter remembered with sadness how Jameson had looked so desolate when she'd asked if he had children.

"Well, it says that Angela, that's Mrs Jameson, was given a low dose of the cure to halt deterioration of her forearm. This was eighteen years ago, she was just a teenager, and so she only has one prosthesis, but the cure has left her unable to bear healthy, fully formed children."

"Oh, that's terrible. Poor Jameson!" said Deter.

"Sadly, it's a very common tale. You either gamble your chances with FED and hope it leaves you able to live a pain-free life and all your important bits intact or you pay a vast sum and take the cure before too much damage is done."

"Damned if you do, damned if you don't." Deter sat silent in thought. The enormity and desperation of the world she'd suddenly found herself in was overwhelming. She still couldn't understand how she could be so sheltered and blind all these years, but it had obviously been Amery's job to keep her in the dark. She felt exhausted, but she wanted to know more. What about her own role? What were the Establishment's plans for her?

"I suppose, then, that you and the Faction are right. A vaccine should be created, but surely the Establishment would have thought of that?" Deter said as she turned to Lincoln for an answer.

"So you'd think, but the Establishment refuse to discuss it. If they are working on something, then they are taking their time to get on with it! I'm confident that the team we have can produce a vaccine within five years."

"Who's on your team?"

"Not even I know that. My role is just to keep the live specimen healthy," he nudged her; she rolled her eyes, "And obtain all the requested samples."

"Who does know?"

"I think Angus does. He's the unelected leader of this division."

Deter looked alarmed; the Faction sounded bigger than she realised. "How many divisions are there?"

Lincoln sighed and pushed his sleeves up. "Loads! The divisions are known as 'pods' and there are lots of little pods all over the world. Each pod tends to be self-sustaining but is united by cause and tries to work together when needed."

Deter needed more answers; at present she felt no affinity to either side as she felt used by both. Until she had the full picture, she couldn't decide where her loyalties lay.

She felt betrayed by the Establishment for keeping her isolated and ignorant, like a princess in her tower of privilege, and disgusted by the Faction for violently kidnapping her and keeping her imprisoned as a lab rat. She was incredibly grateful to Lincoln for answering her questions and being so kind, and it also helped that he was incredibly cute, in a geeky kind of way.

Both preoccupied with their thoughts, they didn't hear someone at the door until the handle was being turned.

"Nice to see you regard the Immune's security as a top priority." Hugo was in a biting mood as he slung a bag down onto the floor. "We're back, not that you noticed we'd gone, since you're all cosy down here with this freak."

"Lovely to see you too, Hugo," Lincoln countered. "Deter has been assisting my research and I'll be updating everyone later."

"Oh, I can't wait!" Hugo snapped sarcastically. "Angus wants you upstairs for prayers and an emergency rebrief and I have ten boxes of pizza." He slung the bag over his shoulder and left, banging the door. As his footsteps receded, they heard him shout back, "And get a lock on that door."

"Prayers?" Deter raised an eyebrow quizzically.

"Yes, of course! We believe in asking for guidance from God every day."

"Seriously? Pizza, prayers, then a quick battle strategy!"

Lincoln smiled. "It's prayers first, then pizza! Yes, it's very much part of many of our lives. Not all, but we have so few expectations in this world, we hope and pray that there's a higher purpose."

"Well, *I* hope it puts Hugo in a better mood," Deter said.

"Sorry about that. He's always miserable when he's hungry. Carrying all those pizzas back must have been torture. They do smell good!"

Lincoln packed up the computer as Deter protested, as she didn't want to be left alone again, "But we haven't finished, we still need to find out what the Establishment is planning and what they intend to do with me?"

"I know, I'll be back as soon as I can. But if Angus has summoned me, I have to go," Lincoln said.

Frustrated by unanswered questions, unsettled by the religious element driving the group and tormented by the delicious smell of pizza that now filled the room, Deter flung herself on the bed angrily as Lincoln carefully locked the door behind him.

Deter rolled over onto her side and felt something digging into her hip. She rolled back the other way and felt her jeans cautiously to inspect the lump. Inside was a small, prettily wrapped parcel about half the size of a ring box. She had forgotten all about it and immediately sat up to examine it closer.

Pulling off the ribbon carefully, she found a small note in tiny, neat script: "Always with you, love from Jameson and your friends from the Plaza."

Tears filled her eyes as she remembered her life in the Plaza fondly. It seemed a lifetime ago.

Inside a tiny box was a tiny egg. It was ceramic with a metal hinge so that the top part opened to reveal a miniature reproduction of Manhattan, with the tallest buildings in New York standing about a centimetre in height. It was a perfect mini 3D map that looked exactly to scale, all fitting within the diameter of this small circle.

It was extraordinary in its craftsmanship; Deter had never seen anything like it. It was the perfect reminder of home and she had opened it at the perfect time. She squeezed it tight in her fist, shut her eyes tight and whispered Jameson a heartfelt thank you.

AMERY

Amery had been on the phone to Jenny's mum for over an hour. She had hardly managed to get a word in as Mrs Poppe sobbed and ranted, so distraught by Jenny's disappearance.

Amery had punctuated the conversation with 'I don't know's and, 'I'm so sorry's and general 'mmmm's and 'uuhhhumm's of varying inflection and tone, none of which consoled Mrs Poppe or halted the continuous outpouring of distress.

Mrs Poppe kept referring to 'those poor, innocent girls' and made no distinction between the three of them. As far as she was concerned, they were all the same: wealthy, protected and now missing. Amery had no idea if she knew that Deter was an Immune.

By the end of the conversation she had a headache but had made small progress. She still had a list of questions to ask but would have to save them for another time, as there had been no opportunity to pose them. It seemed inevitable that someone, presumably the Faction, would soon contact them and ransoms would be demanded. The Poppes (Linda and Hew), it seemed, were preparing to pay anything, but Amery knew that the Establishment wouldn't condone it. A small pod had been destroyed but no sign or link to the girls was discovered. Meanwhile, random memes on social media had appeared, featuring blurred-out, unidentifiable female bodies with the captions 'The Complete Conspiracy' and 'The Tangled Web of Immune Intrigue'. The origin of the pictures was untraceable as so many people had reposted and shared them. Amery was sure one of the pictures was of Deter, but she couldn't be sure. There was talk of a super race and an Immune breeding plan and live chat streams were full of debates about the future of the human race. After so many years of resignation and relative apathy, it felt as though a wave of unrest was slowly gathering momentum and Amery feared that a tsunami was heading towards them.

Amery's next plan was to contact the Lithgows. Padma's parents were both partners in a top Internet-based advertising broker. They bought up space on top networks and sold it to the highest bidder. Gail and Andrew Lithgow were one of the biggest employers in New York, running their trading floor like a stock exchange. Getting hold of them wasn't easy as they had ridiculously long working hours and it wasn't until 10pm that Amery received a call back from Andrew.

"Thank you so much for calling, Mr Lithgow, have you heard anything? I spoke to the Poppes this morning, but they are in limbo like me waiting for news," Amery said.

"It's the same here. Drew, head of security, has assured us that they are making progress and that they are closing in on the Faction."

"Yes, I heard that too." She hesitated. "Mr Lithgow, would you mind me asking you if you've had any connection to the Establishment before now?"

"What do you mean?" Mr Lithgow's voice took on a hostile tone.

"Well, I'm wondering if there was any motive to take the girls other than their wealth? We all suspect this is a straightforward kidnapping, but what if it's more complicated than that?" Amery said.

"I have no idea where you're going with this, but if you're accusing us of—"

"Please, Mr Lithgow, I'm not accusing you of anything. Quite the opposite." The conversation was not going how Amery was hoping. The stress was making it hard for her to express herself and the last thing she wanted was to offend anyone.

"I'm so sorry. But there's something you need to know about Deter, and I'm wondering if Jenny and Padma's situation is linked in any way."

The silence on the end of the phone was slightly unnerving, but Amery continued, "You ought to know that Deter is an Immune."

There was still silence.

"Mr Lithgow? It's just that I'm not sure how much you've been told. It seems we've all been kept in the dark as I was given the impression that Jenny and Padma were too. I've only just learnt that they're not."

"We already knew that."

"Oh!"

There was another long, awkward pause.

"If that's all you rang to say."

"Yes, well. I'm just trying to piece everything together and—"

"It's been a long day, but thank you for calling." Mr Lithgow put the phone down.

So they knew. If they knew, why did they know and to whose benefit? And why was she led to believe they were all Immunes? There didn't seem to be any clear reason.

Amery's headache had reached unbearable proportions. She left her room in search of some pain relief tablets.

MARIA

During her lunch break, Maria checked her social media feed. She posted a picture of herself looking tired, clutching her cleaning equipment with the statement, "Deadbeat Dad, I will find you and one day you will pay. From Downtrodden Mum."

Every now and then, her old friend and ex-neighbour would send news of Ian's latest holiday or new car. It opened old wounds but refuelled her for the fight she knew would come one day. It had been four years now and she hadn't been able to make direct contact with him. Selina had no idea that he had married someone else. All she knew was that he was in England, possibly still in the small village near his elderly parents. He had been ordered to pay child maintenance, but she hadn't received a penny.

"Bastard!" she exclaimed.

"You too!" came a cheery voice from behind her. "No guesses who you're talking about! Have a look at this, this'll take your mind off him." Bonny helped herself to a biscuit and showed her a news article: 'Complete Controversy'. "Everyone is talking about this. What do you think? Are there such people with natural immunity and if so, why haven't we heard about them before?"

"Maybe... Who knows what's been covered up? It's like the cure, they weren't exactly honest about the side effects," Maria said.

"I don't think they knew the side effects." Bonnie didn't mind speaking with her mouth full. She nudged Maria. "Just imagine, though, if it was Selina who was an Immune. It would come with such mixed feelings. You'd be so thankful that she wasn't ever going to be ill and with that would be relief that you wouldn't have to face medical bills you can't afford. But on the other hand, you'd be terrified she'd be outcast or deified and then she'd be whisked away for testing."

Maria eyed up the biscuits. "What are they saying happened exactly?"

"Well, no one's actually seen it. But they are saying that one has been found and rescued from the Establishment," Bonnie said.

Maria shook her head. "So it's all just hearsay and no one has any proof either way?"

"No, not really, but it's thrown up all sorts of questions. Lots of what-ifs." Bonny helped herself to another biscuit. She continued talking, spitting crumbs. "What if an Immune was discovered? What if they could use it to breed out our susceptibility to FED? What if the government has manufactured this superior race? And what would that mean for us?"

Maria was listening, but she was also looking at the biscuit tin and wondering if the teaching staff would notice if a few more went missing. While Bonnie continued reading bits out loud from her news stream, Maria pocketed four biscuits and pushed them down under her phone and keys.

There was always something on the news to gossip about, usually involving the Faction and their endless conspiracy theories. This one about the Complete was slightly more extreme but nothing new. Maria was more preoccupied by her day-to-day worries. Never having enough money being the primary focus, and planning tasks for Selina, ready for their home tuition sessions when she got back.

Maria finished her first cleaning shift at the school by 8am and often came home with small items she had managed to steal: pencils, paper, a stencil set of farm animals that had been behind one of the cupboard doors for a whole term. Anything clearly unwanted or that had fallen down the back of shelves, she carefully hid in her big apron pockets.

She then spent the morning with Selina on schoolwork and then left her at lunchtime with a snack and homework while she went back to school to help with serving lunches. No one she cleaned with knew she also helped in the canteen and no one in the canteen knew she cleaned. There was an unspoken snobbery on both sides. Each feeling they were the superior role and each moaning about the other.

"Oh, the bloody dinner ladies have left a horrible mess by the recycling. Looks like someone spilt something and couldn't be bothered to clear it up!" Bonny would complain.

"Why the cleaners always miss this corner by the recycling I'll never know." The catering manager would gripe, while stacking more empty tins on top of the pile, which would eventually mean more food would slowly drip onto the floor.

The afternoon was spent marking Selina's homework and talking it through. Then Maria had time for a brief nap before job number three. This was not at all hard physically, unlike the other two, but much more demanding in other ways. She worked for Andy, who she had known for a while. They had once, very briefly, been an item, but now she helped him with his model railway business. From the trains themselves (in collectable digital and analogue sets) to the track, the surrounding buildings and miniature people, they sold it all. People, carriages, all with perfect detail, built on the most popular HO scale ratio of 1:87.

Andy needed help with stock takes, processing mail orders and updating the website. He also had his own vast collection laid out in his basement, which needed maintaining and updating. New special editions would be photographed in situ before Maria uploaded them online. This was a job she loved, even though Andy couldn't pay her a huge amount. Somehow the trains brought with them a calm and slower pace from the past, and Maria could often feel herself sinking into an imagined world.

"We all need toys," Andy would say. "So many people have forgotten how to play. Creativity is like a muscle. If we don't flex it every now again, it withers away."

Maria agreed, although miniature train enthusiasts struck her as being a bit of an odd bunch.

Maria checked her online status. She had ten likes on her 'Deadbeat Dad' post. She made a mental note that she ought to begin a serious campaign soon to force Ian to contribute to their financial needs. Selina was growing up fast and she couldn't protect her from FED forever. If only there was a vaccine.

LINCOLN

Lincoln scrolled through his social media, with Deter peering over his shoulder. He was enjoying feeling her breath on his cheek and lost concentration for a minute before giving himself a reality check reminding himself of his inferiority. Any romantic feelings he had for her were not only delusional but also totally inappropriate.

Deter was following the propaganda campaign with interest, feeling a sense of righteousness that her secret elite life should be exposed. She still felt enormously angry towards the Establishment and increasingly sympathetic toward the Faction. It was so wrong that a vaccine hadn't already been created and she had no desire to be part of a super race at the rest of the world's expense. She leant forward and placed her hand on Lincoln's shoulder. "Do you know what would be really powerful?" she said.

"No, what?" He turned and looked into her eyes, seeing how they glowed with energy. Her hand was still on his shoulder, burning through his T-shirt.

"Me, I should make a statement about the situation and call for support for the creation of a vaccine. With increased finances, we could push the time frame of five years down to much less. If money was no object, how soon do you think it would take?"

"You would do that?" Lincoln was amazed that she could offer such a sacrifice, especially after they kidnapped her so mercilessly. It would put her in the direct firing line and place the Establishment under intense public scrutiny.

"Of course... Come on... answer the question. How long?" Deter smiled at him.

He turned back to the screen, thinking. With Deter as a willing figurehead, the Faction could push for progress and deliver a vaccine in just a few years. He felt a rush of excitement.

"It would take a couple of years at most for a truly safe and reliable vaccine to be created. Just think of the suffering that would end!"

"Let's do it." Deter stood up, finally feeling in control of her destiny. She knew by allying herself with the Faction she had drawn an irrevocable line between herself and the Establishment, but she had no regrets. She felt for Jameson's egg as she paced agitatedly; it gave her strength and she was anxious to maximise the moment and build on future possibilities. "I want a contract between the Faction and me drawn up immediately. I want a key for the lock to this room. I want to be included in decisions that this pod makes and I—"

"OK, OK! I'll ask Angus to come and see you. You can make your demands to him." Lincoln held his hands up in mock surrender.

She stopped pacing and looked at him, her eyes searching and pensive.

"You're doing the right thing. A truly amazing, brave and brilliant thing," Lincoln said. She grinned and Lincoln gave her the biggest, broadest smile back.

MARIA

After the first of Deter's videos went live, the reaction was unprecedented. Even Maria found herself swept into the drama of it all. Deter was being hailed as an avenging angel, destroying the evil Establishment's plans to build a super race. Everyone was talking about a vaccine, and Maria felt herself start to relax as the safety of Selina's future looked as if it was in sight. It gave her a goal to aim towards. Two more years of living like this was achievable. Two more years and Selina could be free. The cost of the vaccine would no doubt be high, so Maria doubled her efforts against Ian. She collected all the negative details of his personal and professional life, and began a bitter smear campaign in the hope it would embarrass and shame him into paying maintenance.

LINCOLN

Still feeling guilty for how they had treated the girls, Lincoln arranged a belated birthday gathering for Deter in his room, with Padma and Jenny as the only surprise guests. Now that Deter was collaborating with them, Angus had agreed that the girls could get together. Their security internally was relaxed, although they increased their vigilance in protecting them. The Establishment was still searching for them and there was no way the Faction could risk the girls being found.

Lincoln didn't stay with the girls for long, finding their emotion at being reunited a bit too much to handle, so he brought them a tray of food and drink, and made a quick getaway. Not knowing where to go, as he'd foolishly given them his room, he left for some fresh air and walked aimlessly for a good two hours to give them time to catch up.

Returning to his room, he found them going over the Establishment's treatment of them. It turned out that all three of them had been kept ignorant of FED, no doubt to consolidate and corroborate Deter's view of the world. An elaborate ruse for what, they couldn't be sure. They had hundreds of questions and Lincoln soon wished he'd stayed outside.

ANGUS

Although money wasn't pouring into Maria's account, it arrived in a deluge into the Faction's coffers.

Hopeful members of the public began donating funds, believing that an end to the world's suffering was in sight. The Establishment refused to comment or retaliate, which led the people to believe that they were guilty of all the negative rumours they were being charged with. As the Establishment kept their heads down, the Faction slowly felt brave enough to emerge and show their faces. Leaders finally declared themselves and challenged the Establishment to a face-to-face.

Angus was delighted and decided that they should put his plan into motion. No one knew that Jenny and Padma were not Immunes. The media focussed on their innocence, but their profiles were eclipsed by Deter's role in the Faction's and the Establishment's power games. So Angus set up three fake social media accounts in the girl's names, calling them collectively the three Graces. He imagined Padma as Euphrosyne, the most light-hearted of the group. He remembered how she tried to keep Jenny's spirits up during the initial few days of their imprisonment with the Faction. Jenny, the most conventionally beautiful of the three friends and the most fragile emotionally, would be Algaia; this left Deter as Thalia. Thalia the goddess represented luxury, abundance and blossoming, which tied in completely with the plans the Establishment had for her. Angus gave great thought to their avatars, choosing Botticelli's painting over Rubens (too much pudgy fleshy and florid colouring) and Raphael (their expressions were too bland, too submissive) to crop faces from. He wasn't sure which one was meant to be which but allocated the pretty one on the left to Algaia, the uplifted face on the right to Euphrosyne and the Grace half-turned with her back to the viewer to the mysterious Thalia.

Jenny was revolted by the revelation that everyone looking after them had limbs missing or sections of their torso replaced. Both girls spent the first days in shock, adjusting to the deception and horrors of FED. They had been so young when they had first shown signs of the disease that they either had no recollection or knowledge of its capabilities. They could understand why their parents sheltered them from the beginning.

"I don't blame them, I mean, look!" Jenny retched again as they all examined Lincoln's chest.

"I know," he sighed unhappily, "I don't like looking at it either."

"Put your top back on now!" Deter ordered.

Her friend's faces were completely white. She wasn't sure they were coping with the shock of the revelations. Lincoln taking his arm off and waving it about certainly wasn't helping either.

"Our poor parents! They must have hidden their own... um... injuries from us. Unless they are like us and were given the cure."

"No, they must be like everyone else. Lincoln says that the cure causes awful birth defects, so your parents can't have had it."

"Unless they're Immunes like you, Deter."

"Oh, yes, I'm an Immune and therefore also a Complete. That's why the Establishment wanted me so badly. I'm the ideal mother of the future," said Deter sarcastically.

"All right, steady on," interrupted Padma. "I'm just making sense of this. So Jenny and I had the disease but were cured before it damaged our bodies?"

"Yes, that's right." Lincoln nodded. "Your parents ensured that you had the cure at the very first signs of the disease. So it's possible you might remember having a temperature, and maybe swelling and itchiness in your ankles, but that would probably be it."

"I honestly don't know." Padma sighed. "But surely we'd see people with limbs missing in the streets?"

"All the richest people—" Lincoln began.

"Like us?" interrupted Jenny.

"Err... yes, like your families, have collected to live in Manhattan, and chosen to try and live without the shadow of FED over them. So prosthetics are like mine, we look Complete and no one really talks about it much, as it's considered almost rude. Plus, you have the added protection of the Establishment ensuring that Deter doesn't know anything about it. It seems from their records, following strict rules set by the professor, she has been kept deliberately ignorant."

"But now we've been given the cure, any children we have might have birth defects?" Padma and Jenny both exchanged horrified glances.

Deter and Lincoln nodded; Padma had quickly made that link as a result of their unguarded conversation. Deter could kick herself and felt awful that they hadn't handled this very well.

"I'm so sorry," Lincoln said.

"It's OK. It wasn't you who gave us the cure and if we were showing signs of FED, what choice did our parents have?" Jenny said.

"Well, that's just it!" Lincoln felt on safer ground now. "This is what we don't understand. Why isn't there a vaccine? It's the first thing the Establishment should have introduced. This is why I joined the Faction. I believe that one can be created and I want to be part of the team that does."

"Exactly, that's why I'm staying here to help with the cause. I mean, who wants to look like this? ...No offence, Lincoln," Deter added hastily.

"OK. Let's move on!" said Lincoln.

Deter placed a hand on his chest, looking at his beating heart. "You're quite remarkable. You know, in a weird way."

Lincoln put his T-shirt back on quickly before she realised that she'd made his heart beat double time.

After Jenny and Padma came to terms with their new world, they decided they didn't feel ready to see their parents yet, as although they knew their actions had been motivated out of love, they felt they had been deceived. They would have liked the choice whether to take the cure or not. The idea of not ever being able to have children was a huge and devastating loss. None of them had been treated badly by the Faction, apart from the initial kidnapping, so they held no grudges against them, even though the conditions were nothing like the usual luxury they were used to. They couldn't help wondering what injuries lay hidden underneath the uniform of each of their hosts. As days went by, their admiration for the soldiers grew.

They decided to release a statement making it clear that their loyalties now lay with the Faction. It was the first time they had had a purpose and all three of them enjoyed putting their exceptional educations to good use. Not knowing anything about Angus's plans, they unwittingly raised the profile of his avatars, as it wasn't hard for the public to make the links between them. Previously, the two wealthy and privileged girls had little sympathy from the people. No one had really cared that they had gone missing. Now, as it became apparent that the Establishment had manipulated their lives, they became unwitting celebrities.

Using the avatars, Angus carefully made insinuations and veiled accusations against the Establishment while painting the Faction in an increasingly glowing light. As time passed and his followers grew, he became bolder and began openly challenging the Establishment from the safety of his anonymity. He had no response back.

Deter herself also challenged the Establishment, asking for answers. She also had no response back.

"A clear sign they are guilty of orchestrating an elite breeding programme and for what purpose? They have obviously been planning this for years, but if Deter is Eve, who is Adam? Plus, there must be Adams and Eves around the world, as it would take more than two people to rebuild the population," Angus said.

Hugo and Angus were holding an informal lunchtime meeting. The soldiers of their pod had doubled in the last week and they needed focussing.

"What if Eve didn't fancy Adam? Had they thought of that?" said Lincoln.

"Well, she certainly won't fancy you! Imagine her perfect body pressed up against your diseased carcass… Oh!" Orion smirked as a pink flush travelled up Lincoln's cheek. "You already have!"

"Let's keep this professional," barked Angus, frowning at Orion. He didn't like the new recruit's attitude. Orion had only been a soldier with the Faction for eight days, but he had already offended several key officers by his tactless remarks.

Without Deter's friendship with Lincoln, the Faction would never have reached the pivotal position they were now in. Angus felt hugely satisfied that they had pushed the Establishment to the brink. The fact that it was his pod that had played such a key role made him even prouder. Their next move would be incredibly interesting. Angus had never felt such a coiling of anticipation and couldn't wait to see how things would unfold. Meanwhile, his soldiers were restless and irritable. The last thing they needed was someone on their own team winding them up.

The food was a huge step up. With extra funding came better rations, equipment and a sense of validation. No longer the repressed underdogs, the Faction grew in confidence. Hugo had finished his lunch and pushed his plate back. A junior soldier rushed to clear it, keen to ingratiate himself. That was a first!

"We need to follow orders and increase our training programme; the rumour is that our leaders want to force the Establishment to retaliate and defend their position or step down. Their silence is not acceptable," said Hugo.

"We are ready, sir!" said Orion with passionate enthusiasm.

"No, we are not!" snapped Hugo angrily. "Yes, our troops are growing in numbers, but we are not trained to top military standard. We have hope, anger and righteousness on our side, but not the skills or the equipment to match theirs."

"We have the cover of secrecy and our leaders are brilliant tacticians." Angus tipped back in his chair thoughtfully.

"In theory, Angus, in theory," Hugo retorted.

"It's true; nothing on this scale has been attempted before. But if we don't act now, we never will. This is the weakest the Establishment has ever been." Angus leant forwards to press his point.

"In reputation, yes, but their army is indomitable. The most we can do is unsettle them," Hugo said firmly.

Hugo was getting on his nerves, but Angus replied calmly and with conviction. "We will play our part, as and when we are commanded. Our leaders are no fools." He turned to address the group as a whole. "Every single one of you is here because you believe that a vaccine is our future and every single one of you bears scars, a physical evidence of that belief. We are fighting not for ourselves but for the future of mankind. This is not how life should be. By the grace of our Lord, the moment for change is now."

As his men cheered, Angus felt a deep satisfaction. He knew Hugo had perfectly valid fears, but it was important to keep up morale. He stood up to ensure he left with the last word. "We will, however, prepare for the worst. We are doubling our training programme and also relocating to new premises. Our leaders have acquired a vast new headquarters and wish to merge their top three pods."

A cheer went up through the canteen. Angus continued, "Yes, we are one of those three. This will all take time but brings us excellent facilities and the best resources. The move will take place in waves so as not to attract attention. Be ready."

As Angus left, he could feel the energy in the room. It felt like walking through bright sunshine.

AMERY

Amery sat with silent tears as she read and reread the file she had been given. It had taken weeks to acquire, but with patience and by slowly and discreetly drip feeding her doubts and fears to her sympathetic colleagues at the Establishment, she had gathered support from one of the professor's most trusted secretaries. Like Amery, Robert had worked there his entire adult life with diligent devotion. Amery had known him since his department became responsible for her workload; he had often passed on instructions to her regarding Deter's day-to-day care and like her, he believed she was the wealthy heiress of the Edison estate. Robert was also aware Deter was an Immune, but, like Amery, thought that Jenny and Padma were too. Considering his position and loyalty to the Establishment, he was hurt by the secrecy surrounding the girls. He had considered himself 'in the know' about everything and it wounded his pride to find out he wasn't. After a bit of digging and a bit of flirting with one of the IT guys he often had lunch with, he located a series of encrypted files. It didn't take them too long to decode and he made several copies. One he kept without reading. He knew he wasn't a good actor and anything he found out would be written on his face. He couldn't risk his boss suspecting anything, but there might come a day when the file might be useful. Another file he sent anonymously to the Faction, and the last he gave to Amery with the warning that he wasn't to be involved.

There was so much to process; Amery didn't know where to start. Her beautiful, precious girl was even more valuable than anyone suspected. She discovered that Deter was one of ten clones from the same source. A clone! She couldn't believe it. The Establishment had always taken a firm stand against genetic engineering; this totally defied their own principles. Not only that, but the Establishment had already activated the previous nine with limited success. Just the thought of nine other girls exactly the same as Deter sent Amery's mind into a spin.

The original source of the clones was a woman called Edison, which explained Deter's surname, but other than that there was very little useful information about her, except her statistics and medical records. Amery had no idea that these clones had existed and couldn't believe what she was reading. There were so many layers of secrecy, and to what aim? To protect Deter herself or to create a multi-layered screen to prevent the truth from surfacing? It seemed the only man to truly know the full extent of the story was the professor himself.

Amery, heavy with the knowledge that what she was discovering would change everything, continued to explore the files. She found out that some of the previously activated clones had reached middle age but failed to reproduce, refusing to find life partners or losing life partners to FED.

Others had detached from the world, finding their immunity too isolating and fearing for their safety. They had obviously not felt protected enough and the Establishment had failed in its duty. Most of the clones had been activated during the same time period, but the Establishment tried a different upbringing for each. Deter was the last one left; it all rested with her. But now that the Establishment had lost control of Deter, how was this all going to end?

Amery knew that before the cure, a violent undercover community dealt in organ 'donation', but it wasn't always clear whether the organs were given freely or stolen. Amery knew this illegal activity still carried on, but it was less prevalent. These had been dark days and maybe every single one of the clones had felt so depressed by the state of the world and pressured by their role within it, that they took their own lives. It broke Amery's heart to think of these desperate, beautiful girls, who would have looked just like Deter. She pictured them all with the same neat, small frame, the delicate features and open, trusting gaze. Amery couldn't believe how tragic their deaths had been, for all of them to have killed themselves was beyond her comprehension. Some had chosen to do this early in their lives and others into their twenties. None had reached beyond the age of thirty. Amery felt a chill of fear clutch at her chest as she thought of Deter's future. What would happen to her now?

In the file, it was clear that by the time Deter was a child the Establishment had formed a clear programme; the clone was to be kept ignorant of their own state, ignorant of FED and to be kept busy with an exclusive education. They must be protected at all costs and kept in high-security accommodation with only screened humans for social interaction. They must believe their lives are privileged but purposeful. *Well,* thought Amery resentfully, *I have played my part, unknowingly and without the full picture. Everything has gone according to plan, up until now.*

The Establishment planned for Deter to be moved to Italy, where a number of wealthy families lived just outside Florence. The aim was to find her a suitable life partner with natural immunity. Inside the file was a list of names, showing various family trees and alongside it a scoring system Amery didn't understand. It was rare to see such a high number of Immunes within the same area, as the number of natural Immunes was very slim. It seemed the Establishment had been monitoring this community for decades and believed that they had just the right specimen to assist their breeding programme. This was a tricky issue, as Amery had always known this was on the agenda. But she had hoped that she could make the transition for Deter as easy as possible. With her to protect her, she had always hoped that Deter would fall in love naturally with the right kind of young man. She had assumed that the same would be expected of Jenny and Padma and that by steering them in the right circles, mutually advantageous matches could be made. But this report made it all seem so clinical. The Faction was right; how could anyone engineer the breeding of humans?

Forcing herself to continue reading, Amery found the various reports from Deter's latest medical test that the professor had carried out. It was clear they were nothing to do with an insurance policy, and everything to do with genetic compatibility. Deter's reproductive health had been carefully analysed, ready for her relocation. Yet again, Amery couldn't believe the extent of the professor's duplicity, but this wasn't even the worst thing. Deter, Amery discovered, was named after the word 'determinative', for as the last clone to be activated it was left to her to 'define, qualify or direct' the experiment. Out of all the discoveries, this was somehow the hardest to come to terms with, as Amery had always told Deter her name meant strong. If Deter ever found out about this, she would need every ounce of her strength to make sense of this. Amery prayed that if ever that time came, that Deter would forgive Amery for her part in it.

Amery closed the file and sank onto her bed in despair. She had no idea where Deter was or if she was safe. The Establishment had been very quiet, refusing to respond to the Faction, but they assured Amery that they were working hard on finding Deter. Considering how precious she was to them, it was unlikely that they would be lying about this, but frustratingly, there didn't seem to be any evidence of anything happening. Maybe they were deliberately keeping Amery out of the loop? She resented not knowing what was going on. Amery debated whether to confront Professor Joseph with what she knew. Just because she now knew that Deter was a clone didn't mean she loved her any less. In fact, it made her feel even more protective and desperate to find her. She was angry with the Establishment for keeping her in the dark, but she understood that she was just one cog in the great big machine. She also could see what a difficult position the Establishment was in, considering the fragile nature of the Edison's mental well-being. They couldn't risk losing Deter and the secrecy was paramount to the success of the project.

Amery had to make a decision: should she continue to ally herself with the Establishment or cut off all ties and risk never seeing Deter again? Partly out of fear, she chose to back the Establishment. Fear for what they'd do if she tried to leave and fear of the unknown. It wasn't an easy choice, but she was sure that eventually Deter would be found and then she would be needed. For no one else knew Deter as well as she did. Yes, she would find Professor Joseph and make it clear she had always been, and always would be, loyal in her service. Maybe then they would include her in Deter's rescue plan.

Unfortunately, the Establishment didn't fully trust Amery. Professor Joseph courteously received Amery, and he willingly discussed all aspects about his hopes and dreams for Deter for, like Amery, she was his favourite subject too. Afterwards, it was decided that Amery would no longer be under Establishment employment. They parted with an understanding that, for Deter's sake, Amery would maintain secrecy and the professor apologetically insisted on her signing a renewed confidentiality agreement. Amery left with mixed emotions swirling around her head, for in many ways she felt she been cruelly cut adrift, but in others she felt huge relief.

Amery spent a considerably unhappy time mourning Deter and feeling unsure with what to do with her life, until a chance encounter with Jameson renewed her faith in the world. His wife had connections to a remote unit based on the Kerguelen Islands. Also known as the Desolation Islands, they were the most isolated place on the earth. This independent community had cut themselves off many years ago in the hope of avoiding FED. The Establishment had not been active within the unit for decades and it now considered itself a free state. A small, close community, the islands had been used since for various experimental purposes and also as a sanctuary. The sanctuary element was particularly seductive to Amery, who just wanted to get away from her old life. Within two hours of meeting Jameson's wife, Amery was so keen to leave she embarked on the first plane for Reunion. From there she faced a bleak twenty-eight-day voyage to the island of Grande Terre, where she would become the forty-fifth inhabitant on the windswept rock.

ANGUS

Angus had five seconds to wipe the blood out of his eyes and start running. The explosion had blasted seven of his troops and knocked him off his feet. The rest of his men started heading towards the cover of St Paul's Chapel, the last stone building still standing. Religion had returned with medieval fervour. The world was an unpredictable and terrifying place, and huge faith was placed in God's overall plan. The church stood separate and strong, a place of safety to anyone caught in the battle between the Establishment and the Faction. *Claiming the age-old tradition of sanctuary should,* Angus thought, *be held sacred by both sides.* The oldest church in Manhattan was over two hundred yards away and the Establishment's fighter drones were coming back towards them. Ahead of him, he saw two more men literally explode in front of him as the drone's weapons issued a finely targeted sonic blast. There were only two drones and, two by two, four other men went down. Scattered by the drone attack, he saw that Hugo had led his troops through a narrow alleyway between old brick warehouses. Angus knew those buildings shouldn't be there. It looked as though Hugo had thrown up the buildings by scattering their hologram grenades, which was a complete waste, as drones could see through the façade. Holograms only deceived the human eye. Hugo must have either dropped them by mistake or he was desperate. He decided to follow, as the drones had veered off, tailing the bulk of his men who were aiming for the safety of the church.

After ten minutes of zigzagging through both real and imagined buildings, with his heart pounding, his legs aching and his shoulder sore from the sweat rubbing against his prosthetics, he realised Hugo was cleverly throwing up precautionary holograms to confuse foot soldiers behind them. It had taken a while for members of the Establishment's army to catch up, but they could now be clearly heard in close pursuit. He checked his monitor and counted twenty enemy soldiers within his radar.

He decided to split off before they got any closer and he planned to double back to try and get to St Paul's to find his men. Switching to his dark blue prosthetic, he fired one fragment grenade at the nearest troops behind him, and then he threw a smoke screen grenade before veering off to the left. He shut down his monitor, so although he couldn't track anyone, he would be at less risk of being traced himself. He knew Hugo would be planning to do the same, as they couldn't possibly make it back to base. The church was their only chance.

Frustratingly, he made several wrong turns but didn't dare risk turning his maps on in case his own whereabouts was discovered. Sweat drenched his uniform and the dust from the heat made it hard for him to breathe. After an exhausting detour that seemed to be at least twice as long as he thought it should have been, he finally made it to the chapel. He approached from the rear gateway, carefully keeping to the shadows. It was eerily quiet, so he assumed his men must be inside already. It wasn't until he made it to the front that he realised his men had not reached the safety of the church doors.

The once-peaceful cemetery was now covered in blood and torn tissue. It was impossible to tell how many casualties had been hit, as not a single body was left intact. The drone's sonic blasts had caused instant pulverisation. The graveyard now had as many dead above ground as below, and the appalling sight left Angus winded. He sunk to his knees, weakened by the devastation laid out in front of him. His men, his pod, even that annoying new boy Orion, all dead. He sat in the shade of the church door, looking out as the hot sun caused the flesh to start steaming in the heat. He couldn't weep and he couldn't think what to do next.

LINCOLN

Following the arrival of a top-secret document, the Faction decided to act. They had no idea where the report had come from, but it was definitely real. Lincoln also discovered that Amery's online file at the Establishment had been closed. The information might have come from her; for her records to be terminated, something significant must have happened. Lincoln decided not to tell Deter about the document, as the contents held frightening information about her history and her role as the last of ten clones. He didn't know how she would cope with such knowledge. For ten others just like you to have lived and died one by one, and now being the only one left, that was too much to process. He could imagine what torment it would be for Deter, as she already felt alone in the world, singled out because of her Immune status. For her to find out she was the only cloned human in the world would only increase her feeling of isolation.

The news about Amery, on the other hand, he felt he

should share, for despite her protestations to the contrary, Amery was still very much in Deter's heart. Amery was the closest thing that Deter had to a mother, so she ought to know that she was now totally untraceable. He paced anxiously, pushing his sleeves up and down in an effort to gather his resolve. He would definitely tell her, when the time was right.

Fuelled by this fresh evidence, the Faction made a forceful challenge. "The Faction issue a direct edict, demanding that the Establishment resign. The Establishment has proved they are unworthy of leading the people through the FED crisis. The Establishment has misused funds and abused the people's trust by engineering a secret cloning programme without the express authority from the people.

The Establishment has failed to provide a vaccine.

The Establishment has failed to provide a safe cure.

The Establishment has failed the people."

ANGUS

In response, the Establishment sent the full force of their troops to flush out the Faction. Caught unawares, the Faction's new headquarters were directly hit. Lincoln escorted Deter, Padma and Jenny to a couple of the panic rooms while Angus's troops tried to draw the enemy off. A second pod was left to defend, while the third was sent to attack the Establishment's headquarters. They didn't get far. The Establishment had been anticipating an attack and doubled their forces. It was a huge blow to the Faction. Angus couldn't believe such damage had been done in just a few hours. From being so sure and strong, he now felt sick with exhaustion. He'd never felt so weak and vulnerable. The shock was unbelievable.

All he could do was sit and pray.

ROBERT

A small meeting was just about to begin. Attending were those who had also attended the crisis meeting immediately after the three girls went missing. Amery's absence hung like the Sword of Damocles over Robert's head.

Robert sat so he could see Professor Joseph on the small platform alongside several of his comrades. To his left, just in front of him were the Poppes, Linda and Hew, Jenny's parents, and next to them were Gail and Andrew Lithgow, Padma's parents. They all looked very calm, despite their daughters' recent ordeal with the Faction. The room was a windowless internal conference room, with very little to distinguish it from any other conference room in the world. Earlier, Robert had helped lay out jugs of water and glasses; now he sat back, a cautious observer. The professor stood up and gestured for everyone's attention. The front row immediately sat up taller, ready to hang on to every word, and Robert glanced across to check that each carefully selected member of the press they invited was there.

"We, the Establishment, would like to thank all of you for attending this meeting. During the recent rumblings of unrest, we have continued to do what we do best and work to forge a better future for all mankind. We do not let anything deter us from our duty.

"Since the moment that our biggest enemy, FED, attacked, we have been working on a vaccine and when that failed, we developed a cure. Let me repeat that clearly and slowly. Our endeavours to create a vaccine have failed. Vaccines work by taking cells from the disease and weakening or killing them so they cannot harm you. It is impossible to kill or weaken FED. We have spent billions over past few decades to try and prove this wrong, but to no avail. The only similarity we can draw on is polio, a disease which is the opposite: for that we have a vaccine but no cure."

The professor paused and immediately one of the reporters leapt to fill the silence. "The cure is a matter of contention, Professor. I visited Matthew's Maternity Unit three weeks ago, where over seventy-five per cent of embryos have 'irreconcilable' defects. Every one of those babies was euthanised before their first breath. Huge majorities don't even reach full term. In a population that is already in crisis of extinction, how do we overcome this?"

Robert saw the Lithgows exchange glances with the Poppes. This was obviously the main issue for their families. Padma and Jenny were their only children, and both had received the cure at early stages of the disease. The likelihood of them bringing healthy offspring to full term was incredibly low.

"I'm glad you brought this up," responded the professor. He smiled calmly at his associates, who didn't look as though they agreed at all.

Having carefully selected members of the press, they had hoped for no embarrassing interruptions. Robert made a note to ensure that the young hack was struck off their guest list.

"The cure is not perfect. But it halts the disease and spares you from a life of disability. You," he pointed directly at the reporter, "what parts of your body did FED take? And you?" He pointed to someone else. "And you, and you?" Not waiting for a reply, he pushed his point home. "Everyone here has been affected. My left leg ends above the knee and my right foot is made of plastic! What wouldn't I give to be able to leap out of bed in the morning! But you're right, the cure isn't perfect. But it will be! Thanks to renewed investment, we hope to be able to offer a cure with no side effects within the next two years. It will be safe and it will be free to those on minimum wage. We cannot let anything come in the way of progress. Any rebel uprisings will be met with the same force as yesterday's action in downtown Manhattan. Our message to you is simple: *do not test us*." The professor held everyone's gaze, as though challenging the Faction directly, and then he slumped as though suddenly tired. "In the words of our Lord, forgive them, for they know not what they do."

Robert stood with the rest, cheering as the professor took his seat. *Bravo, Professor,* he thought, *you managed to avoid addressing the issue of clones by focussing on the cure.* Men like him reminded him of why he worked with such a great organisation. For a moment he regretted leaking the file to Amery and the Faction, but then pride kicked in. If they'd confided in him and kept their actions transparent, then he wouldn't have felt betrayed. Besides, he hadn't actually read it himself. He toyed with the idea of opening up the copy he had made; he couldn't help but feel curious, and he wanted to know the full story, especially concerning the cloning. But no, that was foolishness talking, why risk his retirement fund?

He continued clapping enthusiastically and smiled admiringly when the professor's gaze swept over him.

JOSEPH

Satisfied that he had convinced them he was working in their interests, the professor watched as the Lithgows stood and embraced the Poppes. Linda nearly wept with relief. Their precious girls had been found safe and sound in a bunker in the basement of the Faction's headquarters, and Jenny and Padma were currently sleeping after the traumatic events yesterday. The panic room had been rocked by a devastating blast, but the girls had waited until the noise died down before coming out and shouting for help. Establishment soldiers had rushed them off in one of the air ambulances that they sent in for their wounded troops. No one had any idea where Deter was, though. The girls said they had been ushered into a separate bunker as the rooms were small and had been built for just two people each. The fact Deter was missing was a blow to the professor, but the less said about the clone the better.

In return for sustained funding on a significant scale, the professor was turning his attention to correcting the cure.

The Lithgows and Poppes were two of many incredibly wealthy families who offered renewed backing in return for their children's health and well-being. He would find a way to ensure both girls could breed healthy offspring and in return his laboratory would have unlimited resources. It was a satisfyingly rewarding day.

MARIA

The news hit social media within seconds and Maria squeezed her eyes shut as tears of relief poured down her face. They were going to find a safe cure with no horrendous side effects, and it would be free!

Things had suddenly changed for the better and Maria felt a renewed surge of confidence in the future the Establishment promised. Just as they had ridden high in popularity, the three Graces fell just as quickly. Celebrity is fickle, and the girls' images were replaced by the professor's picture in everyone's news feed. Hailed as old and wise, there was no denying his charisma and his stern face with the words '*do not test me*' underneath went viral in minutes.

Maria clutched her frayed cotton blanket around her for comfort and sniffed its comforting aroma. It smelt of Selina and she rubbed it under her nose. Restless after years in quarantine, her daughter had recently been begging to go out. Maria read several articles by mums in similar positions who also kept their children at home, and it was common from around ten years of age for girls to start rebelling. She was so glad Selina wasn't a boy; reports suggested they found being cooped up even more difficult. Most of the schools had more boys than girls and often they stayed safe from FED until mid to late teens. It depended where pockets of the virus lurked. Maria's school seemed to have annual flares hitting children when they were naturally tired at the end of the school year. Many children came back after the summer with new limbs. But equally some didn't come back at all. It was part of life, but if she could keep Selina safe for as long as possible then she would.

She found an old picture of Ian and edited it, making his head look bulbous and slightly deformed. He was still recognisable, but she smirked as she uploaded it to her 'Deadbeat Dad' page. "After ten years of love and nurturing from me, our daughter hasn't even had so much as a dime towards her upkeep from you. Shame on you, Deadbeat Dad, for failing her. Your cushy new life and new wife seem to have gone to your head! Shame on you for putting her before your own flesh and blood!"

As she sat nibbling a biscuit, she watched as friends interacted with her news feed.

"Feel for you, babe."

"You deserve better!"

"Disgusting how he's treated you."

"Shared."

She felt her actions were validated, as each like and comment reinforced her determination to extract maintenance from Ian. She licked her finger and picked up every single dropped crumb from her biscuit.

DETER

The blast was deafening and for a moment Deter was completely disorientated. The sound wiped out her other senses and time seemed to be suspended until both she and Lincoln hit the floor hard as the impact of the explosion knocked them off their feet.

The door of their panic room was still shut, but the corner of the room now had a huge hole and dust was beginning to rain down on them. They moved to the far end until the building stopped moving and waited to see if the attack continued.

"I thought the whole point of a panic room was that it was completely safe."

"Nothing is totally bomb-proof, but our biggest problem now is if they use CO gas. You can't smell it, or see it, so there's no warning," Lincoln said.

"Well, let's not wait here then, let's go."

"But if we go, Deter, we have nowhere to run! The next nearest pod is hundreds of miles away and we have no maps, no money, no plan!"

"If we stay here, we'll be picked up by the Establishment or killed by invisible gases so let's go, now!" said Deter.

Still grumbling about being unprepared, they both climbed up and out of the jagged hole into the ruins of the Faction's pride and joy. A relentless hum of a spy drone sent them running for cover and they hid behind the huge, circular, upturned table, where bold, brave meetings had once been held. Chairs were scattered, upended and smashed against the cracked floor that suddenly gave way and disappeared into a deep crevice. The floors from above had crumpled and flattened, tipping and tilting over each other until the twenty-storey building was reduced to a pile of rubble. As they emerged from the debris, Deter saw how lucky they were that the panic rooms hadn't been completely submerged by the rest of the building. They had been saved by the strength of the central ground floor pillars in the vast reception rooms that had refused to give way. The pillars to the edge of the building had buckled under the weight, tipping all nineteen floors above to one side.

"This is horrendous! Where are the others? Where is everyone?"

Deter looked around in horror, but there was no sign of any survivors.

ANGUS

"Go away!" Angus screamed. He picked up a stone and threw it hard at the small creature. All his grief and anger ricocheted off the marble headstone, splintering into smaller harmless pieces. Realising he'd missed, he roared at the animal, who sat down, his high-pitched whine drilling a hole in Angus's thoughts.

Angus had been sitting in the chapel door for hours, the past running through his head at an increasing speed. Backwards, forwards, faster and faster, then backwards again. Was this how his days were to be measured?

This noisy little dog had been interrupting his tortured mind and he just wanted it to disappear. He wanted his memories to disperse too and if he knew where it was safe to go to, he would travel to wherever that safe place was. As the evening fell, it began to grow as cold as it had been hot in the day. Angus still couldn't move. A few civilians had passed by, but seeing the damage and the fatalities, they had walked swiftly on. No one had come to clear up his comrade's bodies, and the smell was inviting stray dogs and foxes to investigate. This little pup no doubt was as hungry and lonely as he was, but Angus kept vigil, throwing stones to keep the scavengers at bay.

He must have fallen asleep at some point, as urgent barking from the puppy woke him. It took a minute for his eyes to adjust, but he could see movement at the far end of the graveyard. The dog startled whoever it was, and they froze, but Angus could just make out their silhouette. After a while the person began moving again, and Angus shivered as he realised it was probably a Harvester reaping what he could from the remains. He laughed to himself; it was as God willed and this nightmare was part of a higher plan.

The dog was still agitated by the visitor, so Angus reached out to silence it. He had intended to break its neck, but as soon as he touched it, the pup looked directly at him so trustingly. It stopped yowling and licked his hands instead. He watched as the pup washed his hands, cleansing him of the filth from battle and sweat of despair. Once it had finished, it sat next to him on the church steps and together they waited for a new day.

DETER AND LINCOLN

Lincoln pushed Deter further behind the storage locker. They were in a maze of units, some free standing and some in rows. The facility was a mix of modern blocks and huge, rusty boxes. They were looking for somewhere to hide for the night, but security was tight and the layout confusing. This storage business had space for everything, from huge, climate-controlled garages with room to park a bus, to smaller mesh cubicles the size of a dog cage. They stopped for a while between a massive locker and fleets of vans, as Deter was exhausted and they assumed the vans were parked for the night. It was a quiet and sheltered resting place and they didn't intend on staying long. Unfortunately, they didn't notice the security guard until he switched a van's headlights on. They were briefly blinded by the glare, and then ran as fast as they could into the maze of lockers.

"Quick, follow me." Lincoln headed for the darkest corridor he could.

"I can't see!" Deter struggled behind. "Oh!"

"What?"

"Did you see that?" She pointed up, as above them something glinted. "Cameras."

"Damn it, of course, there's nowhere to hide."

They pushed on through the neat and modern lockers until they reached older rusting containers, impenetrable walls stacked high. Still the guard pursued them, his flashlight the only clue to his whereabouts. Above them cameras swivelled, their lenses catching in the torchlight.

"I can hear the cameras as they rotate, he'll find us easily." Deter looked anxiously over her shoulder.

"You must keep going, I'll distract him." Lincoln stopped, his over-exerted heart was making him feel faint; he wasn't used to so much adrenaline rushing though his body.

"Go where? I need you with me; we need to get to somewhere safe so we can figure this out. Together." Deter tugged at Lincoln's shirt. "Come on. I'm not going anywhere without you."

They pushed on, weaving through the giant boxes, looking for an exit.

"Look, that unit has its door open, we could hide in there." Deter pointed.

"But he'll see we've gone in there and shut us in."

"We don't have much choice; we can't run forever."

"Hang on, I have an idea! Where's the nearest camera?" said Lincoln.

They looked up and located two nearby.

"I'm going to climb up and disable them; meanwhile, I want you to run past them. They have motion sensors, so they'll pick you up as you go by. They won't be able to sense me as well if I approach them from behind. They aren't that quick. If he's tracking us live using an app then he'll see you and follow you. Once the next cameras have picked you up, double back and lead him here. We'll both be off grid so then he won't know where we are. Run past this locker and he's bound to assume you've gone inside. With luck, he'll go in and we can shut him in," Lincoln said.

Deter looked carefully at Lincoln, listening to his instructions and noticing how pale he'd become. He was not like Angus and Hugo. They were well-built and strong, with defined muscles and quick reflexes. They spent hours working out and training, proud of being the Faction's army leaders and poster boys. Lincoln was nothing like them. He was a thinker, a science geek, not an action hero. She had no idea if his plan would work, but it was the only plan they had. *Let's just hope I have enough energy to outrun the guard and that Lincoln can climb up to the cameras without being seen.*

"If…" she began, leaning in to rest her hand on his shoulder. "If we don't—"

He took her hand, reluctantly pushing her away. "Beautiful and moving though your goodbye speech would be, I'm afraid we don't have time." He smiled as he turned away and began climbing up the nearest locker. She took one last look and sped back the way they came.

She was breathing hard and beginning to think she was lost when she caught the guard's flashlight out of the corner of her eye. He was nearer than she thought and so she ran towards the light, banging into the lockers to attract his attention. He suddenly turned the corner, so he was right in front of her with the full beam of his light on her face. She pivoted and skittered back the way she'd come. Her heart was beating so loudly, it was all she could hear, and it hurt to breathe she was pulling air in so fast. Just one more block and then they'd be off camera. For a minute she thought she'd gone the wrong way or already missed the locker with the open door. But there it was. She turned off so that they would approach it from the side. That way she could run past the open door without the guard seeing that she didn't go in. She prayed that Lincoln had managed to do his bit and was waiting behind the open door, ready to slam it shut.

Everything was going well, until she slipped. Not only had she taken the corner too fast, but also something had tripped her up. As she fell, she caught her head on the metal wall of one of the lockers. She screamed as the pain felt like a gun exploding in her head. She was aware of Lincoln shouting through the pain as she quickly lost consciousness.

MARIA

As Maria pushed through the door to her flat, bags first, she could feel at once that something wasn't right. Usually Selina would be in the hallway waiting, having been alerted by the sound of the key in the lock. She wasn't in the small sitting room where she did her schoolwork, so Maria dumped her bags on the kitchen table and looked in Selina's bedroom. The smell of this morning's pancakes hung heavy in the air, throughout the flat and anyone following Maria would also pick up a definite whiff of worry as she looked for her daughter. Maria inspected all the rooms, calling out for Selina as she opened wardrobe doors and pulled curtains aside, but she was nowhere to be found and Maria's feeling of slight apprehension escalated to full-blown panic as she realised that her baby definitely wasn't in the flat. If only Ian were here. She didn't know what to do. Who to call first? Her work colleagues weren't close friends and she didn't even know how to contact them. Andy was the only person who might be willing to help. She called him as she paced the hallway.

"Andy, I'm not going to be able to make it later, Selina's gone missing."

"Missing?" Andy repeated.

"Yes, I've just got in after my lunchtime shift and she's not here. I'm slightly later than usual as I stopped at the shops on the way. But she's never left the house, not with me or without me, she's probably lost." Maria could feel the panic threatening to overwhelm her as she imagined her little girl wandering the Harlem streets on her own.

"You don't know she's on her own, maybe someone called round to take her out," Andy said.

"But who? She doesn't know anyone, and everyone understands that quarantined kids must be left alone, and anyway, she's too sensible to go off with anyone without telling me," said Maria.

"Give it a few hours and I'm sure she'll turn up, you said she seemed restless recently, I expect she's just testing her boundaries, both physically and metaphorically!"

"I'm sure you're right, I'll wait until it starts getting dark before I call the police."

"They won't do anything. If you were white, they'd be out scouting the streets immediately, but a little Latin American girl from the wrong end of town will only get a reference number. Give her until five and if she's not back by then, call me and I'll alert the rail fan community. They are a diligent, patient and thorough lot, so perfect for helping find someone. Don't worry about work, I can manage without you for one evening," Andy reassured her.

"Thank you so much, Andy, you don't know how much it means to have your support. I just don't know what to do." Maria felt weak with helplessness, and so consumed with anxiety she couldn't think straight. Andy's calm, deep voice helped to steady her, and she was so grateful for his clarity and common sense.

"If I were you, I'd make a list of all the places she knows about that she might be curious about seeing and then visit each one, asking around if anyone has seen her. Take several photos, the more true to life the better. That's why several are better than just one."

"I will do, that's a great idea. I can't just sit here waiting, I feel I need to do something."

"The only thing is, what if she returns while you're out? Does she have a key?"

"Not officially, no, but she might have taken the spare key. I'll have a look in a minute," said Maria.

"Plus, if she gets back and you're not there she might worry. You'd better leave a note for her." Andy thought for a moment. "Hang on, I think I'd better come over."

"No, don't be silly, I'm sure she'll turn up. I'll make a start listing places she could be and if she's still not back by five I'll ring you."

Maria thanked Andy tearfully and then hung up. The first thing she did was check the drawer for the spare key. It wasn't there, so Selina must have it. That was good news, as it meant that she was out through her own incumbency and not as a result of being kidnapped or lured away. Maria began a list of places she thought her daughter might have gone.

Top of the list was the park, as Selina had been asking about the children's playground there. She had seen pictures after doing research into settlement for her geography project. That project had been a mistake as it opened up all sorts of questions about the evolution of the local area: the shops, the different types of houses and the schools. Of course! The school! That's probably where Selina was; she was desperate to meet other children.

Maria flung on her coat and grabbed her bag off the table. The school was about ten minutes away and she kicked herself for not keeping an eye out earlier when she'd left after her lunch shift. Selina could have been hiding anywhere and Maria could have walked right past her. She just hoped that Selina hadn't been out too long; she had kept her safe for ten years and she wouldn't be able to bear it if after all her efforts her precious baby caught FED. Not now, when the Establishment was so close to promising a new cure.

DETER AND LINCOLN

When Deter awoke, she was first aware of the mother of all headaches, which made it hard for her to open her eyes. The brightness of the room made the thudding even worse. All was quiet and still, and she was in a small but comfortable room with a warm, musty smell of pine floorboards and old books. One whole wall housed an impressive paperback collection of old Penguin classics of fragile first editions, including fiction in orange, biography in dark blue and crime in green. There were a few yellow books and a handful of grey, but only one red, a collection of plays including one: *A Marriage Has Been Arranged*. She carefully opened the glass door, picked it up and opened it. *Blimey*, she thought, *published in 1937, that makes it incredibly rare and valuable*. Probably too much for her to risk damaging! She replaced it carefully in its allotted space and looked around at the rest of the room. It was obviously a study as there was a desk covered in scribbled notes and a wonderful juxtaposition between high-tech screens and old, illustrated reference books arranged haphazardly.

Bright Kilim rugs and throws covered the wooden floor and furniture. They added to the cosy feel of the place and made the sofa she had been resting on firmer but a bit scratchy on her skin. Despite the musty smell, the place was spotlessly clean and the light coming in was filtered slightly by plastic coating on the small window.

Sitting back down on the patterned sofa, she tried to remember what had happened. She had no idea whose room this was, but it had a non-threatening atmosphere, so she didn't feel too worried. Besides, her head hurt so much she couldn't focus on anything else for long. She shut her eyes and dozed off for bit until she was woken by voices in the room next door. Standing up slowly to avoid feeling giddy, she opened the door to find Lincoln sitting at a big kitchen table drinking coffee and chatting to a young man who she didn't recognise.

"Deter, you're awake, how are you feeling?" Lincoln pushed his chair back to greet her, anxiously scanning her face.

"Don't fuss!" she snapped as she tried to pull the chair out from the table. It was heavier than she thought.

Lincoln grabbed it and guided her towards it. "Sit down and look at me." He flashed a light into her eyes, on and off to gauge her pupil reaction. He smiled. "You'll live! Luckily the bump on your head is a simple closed fracture, so nothing that a cold compress can't cure." He turned to the young man, who was sitting watching from the other side of the table. "Do you have a frozen bag of peas?"

The young man got up. "Probably, although they may have been there a few years."

"Just as well I'm not eating them then," grumped Deter. "I'm fine, really."

She paused, and then looked at Lincoln searchingly. "I don't remember anything, though. Where are we?"

The young man handed Lincoln a frosted bag of peas.

Lincoln felt the lump on the back of Deter's head and then applied the makeshift compress. "At Arne's." Lincoln indicated to the young man, Arne, who smiled warmly at her. "We were running through the storage lock-ups by the docks trying to escape the security guard, but then you fell and knocked yourself out."

"Why were we running? I can't remember." Deter frowned and shook her head, hoping to put a firm grasp on her hazy last few hours.

"The Faction building was bombed by the Establishment. There's nothing left... it's hideous! We were lucky and hid in one of the emergency bunkers when the first strikes were made. We basically ran, with no clear plan or idea of what to do next. When the guard discovered us, our instinct was to keep running. After you fell, I had no choice but to try and protect you from him," he smiled as he gestured to Arne, "but luckily he had an understanding boss."

"How? I don't understand. He's the security guard, isn't he?" Deter struggled to follow.

Lincoln reached over to hold her hand. "No, this is Arne; he's the night manager at Howard's Storage. When the guard brought us in, Arne recognised you and wanted to help get us to safety."

When Deter had fallen, Lincoln had been torn; his instinct had been to fight the guard, but he knew he didn't stand a chance. The man was nearly seven foot of pure muscle and Lincoln was not a warrior and already exhausted. He'd let the guard pick Deter up and fling her over his shoulder like an unwanted hoodie on a hot day and he'd followed meekly into the Howard's Storage office. Arne's face had been unreadable as he assessed the situation; he had seemed almost bored by them, until the guard had been dismissed and suddenly it became clear that Arne had known exactly who they were. At least, he'd known who Deter was.

Lincoln paused, pouring Deter a glass of water.

Arne smiled. "Honestly, you can trust me. I have been following your story online and it's an honour to meet you and have you in my home. You've been a much-needed beacon of hope for our lost humanity. To think that there might be an end to mankind's suffering thanks to a well-overdue vaccine... It's incredible!" Arne gazed at her with reverence and a tear in his eye.

"Oh my God, you're a complete nutter!" Deter exclaimed before she could stop herself.

"He's not a nutter!" Lincoln interjected.

"But I am nutty about Completes," Arne smiled, "especially Immune Completes!"

Deter groaned.

"This is how much you mean to people," Lincoln explained. "This is why I've dedicated my life to finding you and hopefully creating a vaccine. You have no idea how FED has destroyed not just our bodies but also our futures. People don't believe a word the Establishment says, they've lied for too long for anyone to start believing them now."

"You're making my head hurt. I'm not sure what I think anymore. I need to lie down." So much had happened in the last few weeks, she needed time to think it through.

"Take these," Lincoln handed her some pills.

"What are these?" she asked suspiciously.

"Just a couple of painkillers for your headache. Have a rest, try and sleep, and we'll make plans later."

Deter looked at him more closely. "You look like you could do with a lie down too." She tried to smile at him, but the effort made the result more of a grimace.

"I've been waiting to see how you are. That knock on your head was a worry, but now I'm reassured that you're OK, I'll have a little nap too." He sighed. All the adrenaline that had kept him going was now crashing. He had never had to push himself physically like that before and he felt quite weak. He knew his heart was on borrowed time, but he couldn't waste energy worrying about it yet.

Deter made her way back to the study and made a comfy nest with the cushions and throws. There was so much whirling around her head: the violent abduction by the Faction, who then turned out to be fuelled by a cause she adopted as her own; the online campaign for an end to Establishment rule, which she led; the excitement as their pod grew to become a huge, powerful force with new premises including state-of-the-art training facilities and science laboratory; the gathering of support from the community as they called for transparency regarding the Establishment's secret plans with Immune Completes at the centre. Then the payback as the Establishment retaliated without compromise. Now there was no laboratory for Lincoln to work in, so no hope of a vaccine. No word from their Faction comrades, who had either been killed or gone into hiding. No sign of her friends Jenny and Padma; who knew if they were safe or not?

It seemed she only had Lincoln and although he was kind, there was a distance. She knew he felt very different to her; after all, she had grown up with a completely distorted perspective, one that was skewed by her ignorance of the true state of the world. Now FED infected her innocent world. Deter sobbed as she felt utter despair. There was no hope.

She slept for over twenty-four hours and during that time Arne left them both resting while he went to work his night shift. In the early hours of the morning he returned to find

Deter and Lincoln back at the kitchen table trying to plan their next move.

"Deter, you can't just go knocking on the Establishment's door! They might let you in, but what if they don't let you out?" Lincoln pushed his sleeves up in frustration.

"Don't be silly! They can't imprison me. I've done nothing wrong! They're the ones who have used me, lied to me and put my life in danger." Deter's head still felt fuzzy and she knew she was being unreasonable, but she couldn't think of another plan.

"They won't see it like that. You're an incredibly valuable asset and you publicly allied yourself to the enemy. I'd never see you again," Lincoln said.

Deter's face softened. She looked at Lincoln, who, suddenly shy, wouldn't meet her eye. She wondered if his heart was beating unnecessarily loudly too.

"Besides," Lincoln said, "without you, I'd be out of a job!"

"But where can you carry out your research? We have no lab now. Everything is destroyed."

"It is here, in New York, but there are other Faction bases all around the world. I just need to establish contact with one and hope they'll agree to my relocation."

"Do you know which might have access to the equipment you need?"

Lincoln thought for a bit; he was trying to remember something. One of the new young recruits came from a wealthy family and when Deter, Jenny and Padma had first arrived, they helped finance the extra costs. Of course after that, money had flooded in, but only Angus really knew where from. If he could only remember the boy's name, he could approach the family for help. Offering Deter, as well as his own services, should be enough for an overseas pod to welcome them, but if they had a sponsor to help with flights and give them references, it would definitely sweeten the deal.

"London. We need to get to London."

Arne stepped forward. "I can get you to London."

Deter and Lincoln looked up, surprised; in the heat of the discussion they had almost forgotten it was Arne's apartment they were staying in.

"You've already done so much for us. We've been doing nothing but eating your food since we got here, well, I have, while Deter's been sleeping." Lincoln grinned.

Arne shrugged. "I'm just so glad to be able to help. My mother died when I was young as she had a terrible infection post-FED. It's quite rare now as ultraviolet light usually prevents infection setting in, but she was unlucky. It doesn't matter that my mum was one of hundreds of thousands to die from FED. Everyone's grief is traumatic and personal to them. I still feel angry and get this pain in my chest when I think about her. Whenever I hear of another family's loss, it just reopens old wounds. No one in this area can afford the cure and we wouldn't take it if we could. There's enough disease already in this world."

"I'm so sorry to hear this, Arne." Deter reached to squeeze his hand and sit him down next to her. "This is why I joined the Faction, as I couldn't believe a vaccine hasn't been created. Lincoln is sure he can use my natural antibodies to help create one, so I don't believe a word from Professor Joseph."

"If you can help us get to London then I'm sure we can find the British Faction, who will definitely welcome us," Lincoln said, full of renewed optimism.

"Why don't you see if you can contact them? Use the computer in the study." Arne gestured to Lincoln, who thanked Arne profusely before turning to start an in-depth search of British Faction members.

"Thank you, Arne, you've been so kind and welcoming, letting us into your home. I've loved sleeping in the study, it's just so cosy, and I love your wall of Penguins!" said Deter.

"Ah, the books! They are all really old and rare. I had to get special UV filters for the glass to help stop them ageing. Some are in good nick, but most have loose leaves from bookworm damage."

"Bookworms! Are they real? I thought it was just an expression for someone who buried themselves in books." Deter raised her eyebrows in surprise.

"Sadly, they are very real. They eat the glue in the spines, which is why the pages come loose. I inherited them and nearly gave them away, as they are quite a responsibility. But I loved the colour codes for each genre so kept them. Then on a whim I had them valued and couldn't believe I'd nearly given away a fortune! I'm missing quite a few, though, I have no purple ones, for example, so while you're in London, keep your eye out!"

"OK! What are the purple ones about?"

"I think they're essays and writing that doesn't fall into the other categories: speeches, letters, for example," Arne said.

"Not exactly light reading, then!"

"No." Arne smiled. "Plus, no one writes their speeches down like that now!"

"It's lovely having beautiful things. I loved my apartment, where I grew up, overlooking Central Park. I had so many things in it I was so fond of and familiar with. The only thing I have to remind me is this," said Deter. Deter pulled out the tiny ceramic egg and opened it to show Arne the miniature city. "It's tiny but really detailed. I look at it when I'm feeling homesick. Homesick for the way things were, if you get what I mean."

"I do, but..." Arne stared at Deter and then back at the reproduction which Deter was still gazing at. "Um... do you know what this is?" He reached out excitedly. "Lincoln?" Calling through to the study, he examined the egg carefully. "Have you seen what Deter's got?"

Lincoln came back in, trying not to look annoyed, as he was just making progress with his online search. "What is it?" He looked at them both questioningly.

"I've no idea, but Arne seems a bit over-'egg'-cited about my miniature ornamental city." Deter laughed.

Lincoln took one look at the egg and gasped. "Wow, you've got a monitor!"

"A monitor? That really doesn't sound very exciting? It sounds like something very strict that tells the teachers when you've broken your pencil, that sort of thing."

"It probably could do that if you programmed it! It's vastly sophisticated and can monitor pretty much anything you want it to. Angus had one to see where each of his soldiers was at any time and what weapons they'd deployed and where. It stays this size for portability but..." Lincoln peered at it closely then clicked a tiny button on the side.

Suddenly, the top half of the egg rotated and then a massive hologram opened out and the whole city filled Arne's kitchen. Deter found herself sitting in the middle of Upper East Side. She got up to stand with the others to see the whole of Manhattan spread out before her. The 3D map was circular and ended before Harlem one way and Midtown the other. It was almost transparent, showing architectural lines mapping the buildings, showing doors, corridors and exact floor height.

"See that?" said Arne, pointing to a small, green light in one of the buildings. "It's been programmed."

"But by who, and what is it showing?" murmured Lincoln.

"There's another!" Deter shouted. "Look, it's right where I used to live! It's flashing green, then amber, what can it mean?"

"Deter, where did you get this from and how long have you had it?" Lincoln said.

"Do you think that whoever programmed it knows that we've activated it?" Arne looked anxious.

"I don't know, but let's close it down." Lincoln switched it off. "Most monitors are linked to their mother, but I don't think ours was on long enough. Deter, come on, we need details."

Deter had never seen Lincoln so worried before. She was completely surprised to find that her sweet little trinket could turn into something like that. "My butler, Jameson, and all the staff at the Plaza gave it to me as a goodbye present."

"Did they say anything about it? Did Jameson say why he was giving it to you?" said Lincoln.

"No, it was a hurried farewell the morning before you kidnapped me, and he gave it beautifully wrapped with this note." She held out a rather crumpled little card.

Lincoln read it out loud: "Always with you, love from Jameson and your friends from the Plaza."

"Always with you… Was Jameson part of the Establishment?" Arne looked suspiciously at the note.

Lincoln saw Deter was about to retort defensively so he cut in calmly. "No, I did a thorough search on him. They had his records, but although he was employed as Deter's butler, he wasn't involved beyond his butlering duties."

Arne frowned. "Good, so long as you're sure, I don't want the Establishment tracking you through the monitor and arriving in the night to blow up my flat!"

"He definitely wouldn't have been a part of the Establishment. He lost two children as his wife took the cure years ago." Deter flushed angrily.

"And he definitely wasn't a member of the Faction either?" said Arne.

"Our three top pods merged recently so I met pretty much everyone. Besides which, I also ran checks on them. Angus doesn't trust anybody," Lincoln said.

"It could still be an Establishment monitor, though; maybe Jameson was given it to give to you. Maybe he couldn't afford to buy you something like this," Arne said.

"Jameson actually has a very wealthy wife. I can't remember her name, but I know they wouldn't need handouts, especially when buying me a gift. I absolutely don't believe he has any links to them except looking after me," said Deter.

"But if it's not Faction- or Establishment-owned, then who the hell programmed it?" Lincoln surprised himself as well as Deter by his outburst, but he felt he was running on empty; he wasn't a strategic planner or soldier and being singlehandedly responsible for Deter was taking its toll.

"Is there any way of linking it up to a computer and hacking into its system?" Arne asked.

"Not without turning it back on, and we don't want to do that until we know if it's friendly, and we won't know that until we turn it back on..." Lincoln sighed.

"So we don't have much choice then, do we?" said Deter flatly.

"No, but we can take precautions. If it's an enemy monitor, then we need an exit plan. Your flat would be compromised, Arne. We would also need to get out of the country as soon as possible afterwards in case they track us down," Lincoln said.

"Or we just dump it somewhere?" said Arne.

"It's too valuable to just throw away! Also, if it's friendly we might need it. Or with the right software I could reprogramme it to our advantage," said Lincoln.

Deter looked at the small replica of the city she loved, so neat, so perfect in miniature. All her precious memories now tainted with uncertainty. "I can't believe this tiny, innocent-looking 'toy' is so much more than it seems." She sighed as she closed the lid and placed the monitor carefully on the table.

They needed to agree a plan and then gather strength until they could move safely to England. Arne could get them out with the next shipment, but they would need to plan the trip carefully. Lincoln could easily pass as a storage staff member if he borrowed Arne's uniform, and with a blonde wig and uniform, even Deter was less recognisable.

"Luckily, most of the guys at work are so bored by the routine that they are just counting their hours, so it's unlikely that you'll arouse suspicion," Arne said.

They were so grateful for Arne's help, not only planning their journey, but also for helping equip them for the voyage ahead. They had fled the Faction as it tumbled down in ruins around them, which meant Lincoln had none of his own clothes or possessions. Deter was getting used to that vulnerability of relying on others but was incredibly pleased with the old but comfy clothes that had belonged to Arne's aunt. In a world where everyone else died of FED, his aunt had managed to drown at a festival. He had simply moved straight in to her flat, keeping her colourful furnishings and the collections of books, as he wouldn't know how to change it even if he'd wanted to. Her clothes were mainly very flamboyant with rich textures in traditional fabrics. Deter found them a bit too exotic for her taste so chose the most subdued, as she didn't want to attract any unwanted attention.

"I have this flat which I live in, and also my parents' house in Connecticut. It was once quite grand, but now that everyone has moved to the city it's too isolated for me. So, I have this huge crumbling pile, over 150 years old and forty-four acres, right in the middle of the forest, slowly turning to dust. I keep meaning to visit, but there's nothing there for me now. I should have gone into construction like my father, then I'd know how to repair it myself, but I chose transport and distribution. How I ended up at Howard's Storage I don't know! At the moment I'm the operations night manager, although, as you know, my hours can be erratic, but I'm hoping to move up to a more senior role with sensible hours."

"Well, we're glad you're the night manager, otherwise who knows where we'd be now?" Deter smiled.

Lincoln spent the next few days looking up known Faction members based in London and trying to keep Deter away from the computer as the news feeds were still full of the cloning story. Someone called Robert Grey had leaked a full copy of the secret file. General public opinion was full of sympathy for Deter, but he knew she wouldn't want it and he felt a sinking helplessness as a few months ago she was a wealthy, privileged girl with not much ambition beyond getting good grades and hanging out with her friends. Although an unwitting pawn, had she never discovered her true purpose, she would have had a simple life of marriage and children in the beautiful Tuscan countryside with a handsome Immune Italian. Lincoln felt huge regret on Deter's behalf as well as an irrational jealousy over the hypothetical Latin lover. He sighed; it was the life he wanted for her, as this one was already changing her into a worn and anxious lesser version. He hoped they would have a few more days with Arne to recover and adjust.

Life within the Faction and then the exhausting flight through the storage yard had left Lincoln often breathless and he was worried how he'd make it on the seven-day voyage from New York to Southampton. Deter was still plagued by headaches and her mood was plummeting. She was often very tired and also pessimistic. Lincoln felt they were both bound by loyalty to the Faction's cause, and hoped they would have the mental and physical energy to see it through. Once they had created the vaccine, who knew what their future could be?

But he couldn't let himself think that far ahead; it would be tempting fate.

There was an unusually cool breeze whipping along the coast when they finally had a call from Arne. He had worked a full day following straight on from a night shift, as the day manager was ill. They had a freight ship leaving in two hours for Southampton and he had only just realised, as his missing colleague had overseen the previous paperwork. Did they want to go? If so, they had better get their arses to the dockyard, pronto!

Donning their disguises and grabbing bags of essentials that Arne had kindly provided for them, they arrived at Howard's Storage, feeling very conspicuous, but soon realised that no one took any notice of yet more porters. Outside for the first time since their night fleeing the security guard, Deter felt a little unsteady. Out of the corner of her eye she felt the blinking cameras refocus on them as they passed by and it made her increasingly unsettled, even though she knew that she was safe with Arne in charge. It took a while to find him as it was obviously an incredibly busy time, but they headed to the main hive of activity on the dock. Arne was checking off a long list which, once completed, he gave a copy of to them. There were porters and sailors loading lightweight goods on board and overhead huge containers were lowered and strapped on deck like giant building blocks. In the centre they were already stacked five high; from a distance it made the ship look as if it were made of Lego.

The documents listed all the cargo overseen by Howard's and included a mix of trading goods as well as privately owned furniture that was being shipped, along with their owners, to a new life overseas.

"OK, I've managed to get you staff quarters as there are only two passengers for this voyage. It should literally be plain sailing, so keep your heads down and if the crew talk to you, they think you are relocating to our Liverpool branch. It actually does exist, so it's a believable story. Be safe, and I'm sorry this is such a quick goodbye. Good luck!"

Deter felt a bit shaky, as it had only been three days since she'd knocked herself out and she still didn't feel quite right. Also, even though they had planned this, it seemed to be happening too fast. She looked even paler than usual as they both embarked the *Vela Star*.

"Thank you, Arne." They both clutched Arne's hands; words could not adequately express their gratitude. In the short time they'd known him, he had been the kindest host and 'bravest conspirator. Lincoln was going to miss having him around. Lincoln wasn't a leader and he missed his team. Looking after Deter was such a responsibility. She wasn't just someone he liked and admired; she was the carrier of their future hope. Her genes had the key to end all mankind's suffering and the responsibility for her welfare rested heavily on Lincoln's shoulders.

ANGUS

Hot sun on the broken concrete flared brightly into Angus's eyes as he opened them onto yet another lonely and disorientating day. Instantly alert and jittery, he removed his thermal control prosthesis which had kept him warm during the cold night and now helped cool him in the bright morning sun. He checked his monitor. It was a futile reflexive action born out of habit and the worry that one of his troops might be out there, alone and in danger. The monitor scanned, sweeping the area for Faction soldiers, but came up empty.

The puppy lay sprawled away from him in the shade of the ruined bunker that served as their main shelter. An empty tin can rattled past him, propelled by a disappointed cat. The puppy went from being fast asleep to fully alert as he spotted the interloper. He bounced playfully, unsure whether to attack or not until he took his cue from Angus, who roared angrily and then, quick as a flash, attached his red-hot firing arm and let go a couple of rounds. The cat tried to flee over the wall, pursued by bullets and the overexcited puppy, but it was blasted into the air as the metal ripped through its torso, killing it instantly. The puppy went wild with delight, making a weird, high, yipping noise and rushed round to retrieve it, and then tossed it into the air, shaking it rapidly to make sure it was definitely dead.

While the puppy played with the cat's carcass, Angus knelt in the rubble and prayed. He didn't pray for forgiveness for killing an innocent creature. He couldn't care less about the cat. He prayed for himself and the future of his fellow man in this messy and unpredictable world. As he prayed, he cried. He cried with hopelessness as he felt the God he was praying to had abandoned him. Where was He? He couldn't see Him. Not in the people he passed in the streets, not in the family he once had, who had died from the effects of FED. Not in the crumbling foundations of the Faction's headquarters that a few days ago were their pride and joy as they rose, feeling invincible, to face the Establishment. He couldn't even see Him in this puppy that was a pathetic mix of needy, demanding and bloodthirsty. But God must have a purpose. When He was ready, He would send a sign.

DETER AND LINCOLN

The *Vela Star* was a long, narrow, three-deck ship with four cargo hatches on the platform deck with the wheelhouse, crew and passenger rooms in the centre. There were also two small cargo holds in the front of the boat. Lincoln and Deter had a small room each at deck level in the superstructure. The two paying passengers were on the floor above which were set below the staterooms. Deter and Lincoln avoided contact with others as much as possible, choosing to stay in their rooms instead of joining the crew in the mess quarters. There would normally be more crew, but as there were only two passengers, the number of staff had been cut.

This was the first time Deter had left the safe and familiar sight of the New York skyline, and she was surprised by the initial delay as the ship negotiated the vast flood barriers. Since industrialisation, years of global warming had resulted in the earth's water levels rising steadily foot by foot. An extensive and costly plan to protect the earth's key cities had begun over one hundred years ago. Now, a ring of three enormous walls circled New York City, encasing it in a protective bubble. It was as though someone drew a circle using the Statue of Liberty as the centre, randomly dividing up communities, slicing through Brooklyn just beyond Brownsville, leaving Queens abandoned to be submerged by the rising water levels. Flowing directly through the city, the Hudson River was kept constantly moderated and monitored. Upper Bay, the point of their departure, was still the heart and hub of sea trade, but only commercial vessels were allowed to dock there. Private boats and pleasure cruises moored on the outer barriers, which doubled as functional floodgates, with short-stay hotels and associated entertainment located within the permanent sections of the structure. In between were barriers that could be raised and lowered to allow ships to pass through in a complicated lock-style system. Similar systems were in place up and down the coast, protecting the key ports and places of historic international value. Some of the highest places, for example Machu Picchu, which were still thousands of metres above the sea, were now repopulated after years of being abandoned. People knew they could re-establish communities there, safe in the knowledge that flooding would never be an issue.

As they entered the last barrier, they waited while water flooded in, raising the ship up to sea level. Above them, several glass towers stood sentry, each with incredible panoramic views, looking down into the city one way and across the ocean the other.

Deter was astounded by the engineering complexity, and couldn't believe this extraordinary structure existed. "This is vast, but impossible to see from the city centre. Even from my crow's nest in the Plaza. The other buildings get in the way, so this is the first time I've seen it."

"There's another one, the other end at Southampton. From there we'll get the amphibus that travels on both land and water. They are usually pretty efficient and with luck won't keep us waiting in the cold British air for too long," said Lincoln.

Above them, they could see people enjoying the view in what appeared to be a gym, as their heads bobbed up and down as though on a bike or step machine.

"Everyone is busy recharging their power packs!" Deter observed.

Lincoln smiled. "Yup! The more power credits you have, the better, and we all have to work for them."

"I've never had a power pack, I've noticed you all have them, but Amery has always dealt with everything, so I don't have one of my own." Deter wistfully tugged at her blonde wig.

"I'm only using mine for reconditioning my prosthetics, which I do weekly, and accessing the Internet, which is vital. But if we stay with people, it's good form to use your own for hot water, electricity and stuff, as otherwise it ends up going on their property bills."

"Oh dear, I didn't know this when we were at Arne's, he must think I'm really rude," Deter fretted.

"Don't be silly, he knows all about you and didn't expect you to know, and anyway, I used mine, and recharged it before we left. I did over five hours on the bike in total, that's the best and quickest way to recharge." Lincoln carried on explaining about the best ways to generate energy and showed her his in-built solar panel on his shoulder blades. She hadn't noticed these before, as they didn't glow through his T-shirt the way his heart did.

"Even the flood barriers have an in-built hydroelectric power plant. Think of the amount of water that gets pushed through every day and the force of it. We are so lucky, living in this city," said Lincoln.

"Well, we won't be any more and it seems that I've spent my whole life in a weird Establishment bubble. I wish I had more time to get to know New York properly." Deter scratched her head; she wasn't enjoying wearing the wig.

"We'll be back, I'm sure, and London is pretty cool, so I hear, and structured in a similar way, but the people and vibe is really different."

"What if we can't find any Faction members to help us?" Deter asked. "The whole terrible battle here might have sent everyone underground."

"I'm pretty sure I can sort it out, as Arne has given me some leads and I remember some names that Angus used to refer to. Let's not worry, and enjoy the fact that we are pretty much forced to relax while we're stuck on this boat. When we get through the barrier, the wind will hit us, so let's go and explore the ship."

Everywhere inside the ship echoed slightly and Deter felt she was stuck inside a rusty tin can. There were no luxuries, not even carpets, and once they hit the high seas, Deter spent most of her days lying on her bed reading the books she found left behind by previous passengers. They were an odd, well-thumbed collection: some leaflets (clearly old Establishment propaganda), a serious article on water properties with the last page missing, and, joy of joys, several big, fat novels… but no first-edition Penguins!

The journey gave them time. Time to readjust and catch up with everything that had happened, and to learn more about each other. They spent their days dozing, and long nights wandering the ship and talking. Sitting on deck with the beauty of the night sky forming a vast cathedral of stars around them, they could have been the only two people left in the world.

But although she felt increasingly relaxed, her headaches less frequent and her energy returning, Deter was haunted by the occasional buzz of a phantom camera. She sometimes even thought she could see the glint of a glass lens out of the corner of her eye, but if she looked again, there was nothing. The long, hot summer was coming to an end and as they crossed the North Atlantic, they felt the first autumn gales blowing around the ship. Most of the crossing was calm but getting noticeably colder as they passed through the Celtic Sea into the English Channel. As they headed towards the coastline, high, austere cliff faces glowed through the grey sea mist as gulls wheedled their way, screeching into the wind. Rounding the Isle of Wight, Lincoln and Deter joined their fellow passengers on deck as they finally pulled into Southampton Water.

Lincoln had used his time on board the *Vela Star* wisely, double-checking his new London contacts. He'd managed to find Pip Arnold, the leader of one of the biggest pods based in Christian Street, Whitechapel, with links to St Peter's research unit. From what he could gather, Pip was a jobbing actor in the day and bartender at night. He had mainly been working as a role-play actor in short disaster dramas for the emergency services, local doctors and hospitals. This had helped build him a considerable network of friends and acquaintances from all walks of life. However, it was owing to his family that he had connections to St Peter's, as his uncle was a research professor. St Peter's, an ancient, noble facility, was set up in the 1970s to find vaccines to combat infectious diseases, especially those originating from and affecting the least privileged countries. They had already started their own independent research into a vaccine but had very little success, owing to lack of funding.

Pip would be working when they arrived, but he had sent his girlfriend Annabel to meet them. All travel in England had recently been restricted to public transport only. Commercial vehicles and emergency services were the only exceptions.

This was a new policy to ration resources, which would, no doubt, be adopted worldwide soon. It was, however, incredibly efficient, with high-speed amphitrains linking all the far corners, and amphibuses running every thirty minutes to and from all towns. As with most of the world, there were only a few villages left. It simply wasn't possible to live in such isolation, as stretches of land were now underwater and the population was so low.

Annabel had fair hair a bit like candy floss, which she had tried to organise into a long braid, but bits had flown free and kept sticking to her face. The wind at Southampton was pretty keen to mess up not just her hair but also all the notes Pip had written for her. In her pocket were small balls of earth, packed with seeds that she took out and threw at cracked concrete walkways.

"What are you doing?" Deter asked as she narrowly missed being covered in a clod of mud that hurtled past her.

"I'm a Garden Guerrilla." Annabel smiled cheerfully, lobbing another brown blob over her shoulder. "There's hundreds of us; it's a tradition that's been going on for years. These are seed bombs." She showed Lincoln and Deter the small earth balls. "These ones are packed with wild seeds, especially red poppies; they're my favourite. You can't have enough poppies. But there are also cornflowers, forget-me-nots, campion, vetch and foxgloves. Bees and butterflies love them."

The wind was getting colder as they crossed the huge open roads. Big trucks were lined up, bringing goods for transportation that the three of them dodged as Annabel led them through a short cut to the massive bus station on the edge of the docklands.

It was the bleakest place Deter had been in; it was a far cry from the warmth and comforting bustle of New York. As they waited for their bus, she had a feeling they were being watched, but the only people there were looking cold and fed up and not remotely interested in her. There was a sudden rush of activity as a noisy crush of extraordinary-looking people rushed through on skateboards. Accompanied by loud hoots and wild cries, they hurtled through the station. People stepped back to avoid being crashed into as the unruly rabble swept through, regardless of obstacles. One of them made a grab for a bystander's bag and missed but then scooted past, laughing loudly at their own antics. Some looked to Deter like children, but then she realised they had stumps where their legs ended, below the knee, and above, plus some without any at all. With or without, they were fast and used what limbs they had to propel themselves forward, flying over curbs and bouncing off stairs. They had no fear and incredible skill.

"Street kids! They aren't as bad as people make out, but they aren't to be trusted." Annabel smiled indulgently as she gently pushed Deter behind her.

The woman who had nearly had her bag swiped was clutching it tightly as everyone tensely watched the skateboarders who disappeared as suddenly as they'd arrived.

"We have shelters for them, but nine times out of ten they prefer living on the streets together. There's so many abandoned properties that they keep warm enough; they only come out when they're hungry. I expect they're heading up to the soup kitchens up on the common," Annabel said.

It wasn't long ago that Deter had found out about FED, so seeing people like this without their limbs was a bit shocking. Lincoln felt guilty for a moment for the other things Deter hadn't been told yet. He planned to reveal the Establishment's file once they were safe and settled, but he was worried. Revealing to her that she was not only a clone, but also the last of ten to survive, might have a negative effect on her. She was still trying to adjust to this new world and there was always the fear that she would decline into depression like the other clones before her. It was clear she had been happy and thrived in the trouble-free world the Establishment had created for her. What if the full truth was too much to handle?

"You'll find England very different from New York," Annabel said cheerfully as she tried to remove a piece of flyaway hair that had got caught across her face. "We are much more accepting of our physical failings, and as a nation we spend more on prosthetics and trying to maintain a high quality of life, whereas America is much more cure-driven. That's why you'll find more Completes in New York. We British, being more cautious and suspicious, waited to see the outcome. Plus, the Establishment here is more lax in their relationship to us. We've got on quite well up to now, as obviously the war in New York has got everyone on high alert. The likelihood of things becoming violent here are slim, though, as our leaders strongly believe that peaceful pressure groups have far more power. To be honest, the Faction over here is really disappointed with how things went over there. Having you here will complicate things a bit and Pip did think twice before offering you a place." She paused. "Ah, here's our bus."

Feeling slightly awkward at this very candid welcome, they stood and watched as an incredibly long, once sleek, but still streamlined vehicle pulled up. It was lightweight and travelled fast over land and water to counteract the flash floods that plagued the country yearly. This one only had three compartments but sometimes they had as many as six. A mix of upright seats with ample storage and night recliners, the buses ran like clockwork twenty-four hours a day.

Annabel led the way up to the top deck on the middle carriage. "I always go in the middle, feel more protected, although there's no statistical proof that it's safer." She chose a front-facing seat with a small table in front of it.

Deter sat next to her and Lincoln slid in opposite after stashing their bags overhead. Listening to Annabel give a running commentary on everything arbitrary that caught her attention as they pulled out of the station, they then settled down for the journey into London and a new chapter in their lives.

When they left or approached cities, they went through a familiar series of flood barriers and passed well-preserved, built-up areas with clusters of low brick buildings. Annabel pointed out the white roof and spires of Winchester Cathedral. Neither Deter nor Lincoln had seen such a beautiful old building before and they were amazed how the city spread out, sprawling in a seemingly higgledy-piggledy way, so different from New York, which rose up, straight, tall and orderly.

The countryside, so green and abundantly full of wildlife, was at times unruly and wild as nature reclaimed the neglected areas. Filling it with tangled, ever-reaching hedgerows, it could also be at times cultivated and closely cropped after the recent harvests. The road stretched on, wide and empty with only more buses and haulage vehicles for company. Every now and then, a single motorbike would whizz past with flashing lights.

"Donor bikes," said Annabel. "You must have these in your country too."

"We have a lot of illegal donations going on in New York, but the majority can't afford it. It's much talked about, but in reality it's pretty rare." Lincoln showed her his prosthetic arms. "We're much more interested in hi-tech breathable skin and the perfect fit. This is about as realistic as it gets. I was working in a hospital at the time and offered to trial these new models. I wouldn't have been able to afford them otherwise. But most kids like bright, neon, customised ones these days."

"Oh, I know! Pip has a ridiculous collection. You'll see when you meet him, he'll be in bartender mode so will have his party lights on, no doubt. I like the natural look myself, but for running I like to get my blades on." She grinned and showed them a picture of herself mid-stride, flashing two purpose-built curved metal sports below the knee instead of calf and foot.

It took an hour and a half to reach Victoria, but they had stopped at Basingstoke and Farnborough where they added another carriage on the end.

"You still have trains?" Annabel asked Lincoln.

"Only just, and those we do have are being phased out."

"I know, the flooding is ridiculous. These buses need updating, look at the state of this upholstery." She picked at the worn fabric on the headrest. "They do still work, though, the water doesn't slow them down at all, although one driver did manage to lose the road and ended up in a field. I think they're going to programme the routes in soon. I'm surprised they haven't already." Annabel stood up as the bus came to a standstill. "OK, follow me and put this cap on, the last thing we want to do is antagonise the Establishment. If they hear you're here, they'll get all touchy." Annabel passed Deter a tweed flat cap, which Deter pulled down over her wig.

They followed Annabel off the bus and began a long, fast walk down into the underground, where they hopped on the District Line until Aldgate East.

Deter pulled her cap down further as they pushed through the throng in the dirty and overcrowded streets. It was the first time she'd taken the underground. It was quite fascinating; there was so much to take in. Deter was starting to feel tired, even though she hadn't actually done much today. Once back up into the open, Annabel led them into increasingly narrow brick roads. They'd hit lunchtime and it seemed as though the entire local population had fled their offices and headed down to sample the incredible selection of street food that assailed their senses. New York was busy, but the streets were twice as wide and the claustrophobic effect in Brick Lane was heightened when, on looking down each side street, Deter could only see yet another similar route opening up.

They passed more people with missing limbs, mingling happily with others wielding a huge range of fanciful creations from the practical to the purely decorative. One man had deliberately attached his leg prosthesis to his arm and vice versa. It was a disturbing effect, somehow more unsettling than seeing people with no limbs at all. Deter had to remind herself that everyone she knew now, apart from Jenny and Padma, had bodies with missing parts. She had tried to imagine Lincoln without his arms, but he caught her looking at him sideways and for some reason it made her blush.

The Faction had taken over a very large but old public house, which smelt of damp but had the remnants of fading grandeur about it, as the old bar area was furnished in opulent style, with swags of fabric and chipped gold leaf mouldings. Still operational and run by the Faction, Pip was coming to the end of his lunchtime shift. A small shop front, with 'The George' written above, the modest entrance belied the massive warren of rooms that led from one to another.

Annabel quickly took them through into a secure private area that opened into a long, squeaky corridor with lots of rooms and more passageways leading off it.

"It's actually three properties built into one. The original pub was quite tiny, but then we acquired the old warehouse next door and now we own the house on the other side. We've knocked doorways through to link everything together and it's handy as we can enter and leave fairly inconspicuously." Annabel gestured for them to mind their head as they stepped through a low doorway into a vast, central space kitted out with small rooms just slung up against the walls like pictures. This must have been the old warehouse. Each of the small box rooms housed a bed and some had personal belongings on shelves and a window looking out onto the huge communal area. Some had shut their doors so you couldn't tell if they were occupied or not. Others had people in them, who looked out curiously at the newcomers.

The floor at the bottom was divided into traditional living areas: a comfy sitting area, a kitchen, and a dining room with a mix of long trestles and small, round tables only big enough for two all crowding in together. It was a welcoming and relaxed atmosphere, but Deter could feel an industrious undercurrent.

"So, most of the rooms you passed are for storing equipment, food, promotional material, that kind of thing, plus we have a few that can be booked for meetings or studying. There are also beds for guests who pass through, but everyone who lives here usually chooses to inhabit one of our wall rooms." Annabel pointed to one room painted a cheerful bright green with pink flowers. "That's mine, but I also share Pip's, and he has one looking out onto the street."

She led the way to the kitchen area. "Bet you're starving! Let's see what's left in the fridge."

Annabel gazed into the fridge while Lincoln and Deter continued staring at everything around them.

They ate an eclectic assortment of snacks, a mix of leftovers from both the pub and street food outside. Still, it was just what they needed, as Lincoln and Deter hasn't realised how hungry they were.

"Pip will be finishing his shift soon, but until then I'll show you to one of the guest rooms. It can be yours for however long you stay, and of course if you decide you don't want to leave, you can always move into one of our wall rooms." Deter had to admit the box rooms were very tempting.

"Worth staying just for one of those." She smiled at Annabel. "Although I think yours is the cutest!"

Sweeping her eyes around once more, drinking everything in, Deter reluctantly turned to follow the others back into the corridor they'd previously walked along. If it weren't for the occasional change in floor and ceiling height, it would be easy to get lost, as the passageway didn't follow the same building rules as her hotel in New York. Centuries of additions, change of use and maybe changed minds, meant this ancient linking aisle was full of character.

ANGUS

As the wind swept through the ruins of the high rise, it lifted the lighter debris, moving it, tossing it, so that the landscape of this urban desert constantly shifted. Swirls of light snow tumbled with the rags of plastic, until the frozen flakes outweighed the fragments of waste and held them down, pinning them to the dusty floor. As the weather turned colder and more snow drifted in, Angus was drawn back to the ruins of the Faction's headquarters, partly out of the need to punish himself, but also he felt compelled to keep checking that there were no survivors.

He was tired. So tired of being watchful and tired of being alone. He knew things would change; he knew a sign would come.

He missed his comrades, that feeling of unity, of someone out there having your back. Sometimes he heard the tramp of soldier's footsteps and, hoping it might be one of his own men, he watched in anticipation, but it was usually Establishment men that he knew were looking for survivors too. It was easy to outwit them, and the puppy was a surprisingly efficient guard.

After the Establishment soldiers had scouted the ruins for the third time, it was clear they had retrieved all they could from the rubble. The Harvesters, who resold scrap, had already collected anything that could be reused and the soldiers had dragged huge sections of debris to the side to access the remains of computer chips and databases from what was left of the office. Angus had watched them from a vantage point on the top of a nearby housing block and laughed out loud as he knew that their efforts were pointless. No information remained, as their comrade Lionel who had remained in the central office during the battle, precisely for that point, had wiped it all.

The damaged bomb shelters offered some protection from the elements, and Angus dragged sections of glass from the windows and large blocks together to build a series of walls to keep out the chill. Crawling into the remains of the shelter, he found a cavity that still had the panic room supplies. Bottled water, tinned food and chocolate bars, blankets, plus a couple of torches were the most welcome sight. He opened a 'deep-fill' steak and ale pie, which he shared with the pup, then curled up where he was and fell asleep.

DETER AND LINCOLN

Tiny traces of the original computer programming showed Lincoln and Pip that the monitor definitely wasn't of either Faction or Establishment origin.

Baffling but intriguing, it was obviously owned by a pretty sophisticated third party with excellent facilities. Monitors were not cheap or easy to programme, and this one covered the whole of central Manhattan. It was really quite extraordinary.

They worked out that the monitor couldn't be activated in England, as there were no cameras to link it to. This was just as well, as until they started opening it up, they had no way of understanding its capabilities. Its main role, it seemed, was to trigger certain cameras when within sight of them. Until then the cameras were dormant. But once activated it looked as though they either began recording or streaming activity. Three hundred cameras were located in New York, most of them in areas that Deter hung out in. Her hotel had ten alone from the lobby entrance to the corridor leading to her suite, but not actually in her rooms. Various cafés, art galleries, museums and shops were also targeted, and Deter knew all the locations intimately since childhood.

"Look! That's the rock in Central Park that I used to have teddy bear picnics on. Amery used to help me pack a hamper and we always had a tiny little teapot that I used to insist on taking, even though it dribbled and couldn't actually hold much liquid. How did they know to put one there? Why would they? This is so weird." To find out she was spied on by the Establishment wouldn't have surprised Deter at this stage, but to discover that an unknown third party was involved was unsettling.

She spent a great deal of time thinking and pacing the long, squeaky corridors and avoiding the other people who, although friendly, seemed slightly in awe of her. There was none of the anger, the youthful outrage that had united her with the Faction in America. Here no one gave too much away of their underlying feelings. It was hard to read them, and she was tired and wanted to go home. If only there was a magic wand to turn back time. Seeing all the camera locations on the monitor had made her even more homesick as they had triggered such blissful childhood memories. When she was little, she used to imagine Amery was her real mum, and in many ways she had been. She was the only person who had given her constant love and affection, cuddled her when she felt sad and laughed with her over silly little jokes, the only person who told her off when she needed to be put in line. She missed Amery so much, but how could she ever see her again, especially after she'd been planning to send her off to start a breeding programme? Who the hell breeds humans? She imagined herself with an unknown man in an enclosure with big glass windows, much like an animal at a zoo. She knew it wouldn't have been like that, but that's how she pictured it.

Two of them warily circling each other with Professor Joseph observing and making notes on their every move. Maybe to encourage them, amorous music would be piped in and a romantic dinner for two with red roses scattered on the floor.

Wincing at the thought, she turned, as she reached the huge communal room with the rows of box rooms strung up like bird's nests around the walls. Retracing her route along the hallway, she thought of Jenny and Padma imagining them hanging out with Asher. She felt a bit sick with jealousy over her old life. She had really liked Asher and was only just getting to know him. There had definitely been a spark, a connection. Not a boom, wow, he's the one moment, but a gentle recognition. Was he a Complete like them or was he an Immune like her? She wouldn't have minded being stuck in a big enclosure with him. But if he had been a suitable mate, then surely the Establishment would have encouraged their relationship? What could be better than two Immunes falling in love without help?

But then, what if he was like Lincoln, though, and under his clothes he had missing limbs? Would she mind? She thought of Lincoln's cage around his chest to protect his heart. He was so fragile, yet beautiful, with incredible strength and determination to survive. He wasn't a warrior, a traditional hero like Angus and Hugo; he was somehow more. She wanted him to take her in his arms and tell her everything was going to be OK. Then she remembered his arms were plastic and not like hers, real warm flesh and blood. What would it feel like to touch and be touched by them? Just as she was thinking of him, Lincoln emerged, looking bleary-eyed from the computer hub and she blushed guiltily. "Oh, hello, how are you getting on?"

"Well, we think we've got as far as we can. To find out more we'd have to activate it and to do that we'd need to go back to New York. Not something I'm planning in a hurry." He pushed his sleeves up agitatedly.

"No... no... me either," she stuttered, following his movement, her last private thoughts still embarrassing her.

"Anyway," he continued, "do you think we should leave the monitor with Pip for the Faction to reprogramme? They could use it for so many things, it would be a huge asset."

"Oh! I hadn't really given it much thought... but it was a present... from Jameson!" Deter was torn. "But I do realise how valuable it is."

"Well, you don't have to decide right now, just have a think about it."

"OK, I will do." Deter frowned, a different concern wrinkling her brow. "Lincoln, can I talk to you a minute, not here, but somewhere we won't be disturbed or interrupted?"

"Of course, what's wrong?" Instantly concerned, Lincoln led her to the nearest private place, which was his room along the corridor.

It was a bland and characterless room, although it had a very small window, with an enormous and deep windowsill, which Lincoln used as an extra shelf. As he had no personal belongings apart from the old device and clothes Arne had given him, it was still pretty much as he'd found it, with the addition of dirty crockery he hadn't returned to the communal kitchen.

They sat at a tiny table in the corner and while Deter collected her thoughts, Lincoln disappeared with the used mugs to quickly make some fresh tea in some clean ones.

When he returned, she tried to explain that she wasn't unhappy, just not happy either. "I just don't know who I am anymore. I thought I was Deter from the Plaza, with the most fabulous friends in the most fabulous city. I was enjoying studying and although I don't have family, I had Amery and

Jameson to look after me, and that was all I needed. The sudden news that I was to be relocated to a clinic was a shock, but I didn't know the reason for it then, but with the revelation of my immunity to the whole FED thing, it's been almost too much to take on. Of course, I'm glad I'm Immune. But I can't get over that I was going to be part of a weird, freaky breeding programme!"

"I know it's a lot to process." Lincoln grimaced in sympathy.

Deter continued, "I was more than happy to be part of the Faction's campaign for a vaccine. It seemed the only answer, but now that new life I was getting used to with you and Angus and Hugo and everyone has also been ripped away. And what happened to Jenny and Padma? I keep thinking, maybe they're dead and we don't even know. There are so many things I just don't know and although everyone here is very kind, I find them quite hard to read. They're not exactly friendly!"

What Deter really wanted to say was that she wanted to go home. She wanted to wail and cry and throw herself on the bed in a fit of pique, but she knew that would be incredibly childish; she didn't want Lincoln to think less of her.

"I just wish I knew who I really was," she tried hard not let her voice rise in a whine, "and who this third party is who created the monitor? How much was Amery involved in the Establishment's plans and what am I supposed to do with my life?"

Lincoln hesitated; seeing him pause made Deter suspicious. "What? What are you not telling me? Is there something you know that I don't?"

She glared at him angrily and as she stared him down, Lincoln felt a huge surge of guilt, which turned him pink with discomfort.

"You do know something! Tell me!" Deter raised her voice and the table she was resting on shook and threatened to spill their hot tea.

"It's not something I kept from you deliberately. You must first know that what I found out was not public knowledge, but when the Faction found out, it's what gave them grounds to push the Establishment into war."

Lincoln talked slowly and softly, explaining about the files that had been leaked. She took the news she was a clone calmly but was upset to find that her name Deter wasn't chosen to symbolise strength as Amery had told her, but was short for determinative, for as the last of the ten activated clones, it was she who was the deciding factor. Only she now had the power to determine the outcome of the experiment. She gave in to her tears as she heard about the short unhappy lives of her nine sisters. She could totally understand how they felt, as she was also experiencing a gradual sinking as her faith in mankind was slipping away. She quietly read the whole file that Lincoln showed her, that Robert Grey had leaked to the press a few weeks ago. It really was true.

So, there were no parents at all. Never had been. The mother she missed never even existed, and her identity as an orphaned heiress had been complete fabrication. They talked all that afternoon, over and over, as Deter tried to get her head around the new revelations.

Lincoln, ever-patient and feeling desperately sad and responsible for being part of the society that had brought Deter into existence, tried his best to unravel the thoughts in her head. He also had to admit that Amery's file had been deleted, which meant she no longer worked for the Establishment. Beyond that, it was only guesswork; she could have easily resigned now she no longer had Deter to care for. There wouldn't have been any reason to stay. Lincoln feared the deletion signalled something more sinister but kept his opinion as upbeat as he could for Deter's sake. They also searched for news of Jenny and Padma, and found that they had new profiles on the Establishment's database, but their social media accounts were not updated. They discussed what that could mean and guessed that after the bombing they hadn't been so lucky in escaping. Deter wanted to try and contact them, but Lincoln pointed out that if they were being monitored by the Establishment, it could give away their location.

After they finished talking, Lincoln gave Deter a couple of pills for her headache and left her in his room while he went in search of food and yet more sweet milky tea. When he returned, she was asleep on his bed so he left and sat and ate in the huge refectory area and tried to answer small talk from comrades as politely as he could, but he felt distracted and devastated for Deter. He went to update Pip and Annabel, as he felt they ought to know that Deter had just found out she was a clone and they were sympathetic and so kind when they saw that he was distressed about it. Pip was getting ready for a shift working in the bar and had his party prosthetics on.

"You can always talk to us, as you have a huge role. She is not just your friend, but the woman who holds the key for our future."

"Yeah, it's pretty tough on you both. Having to flee across the world must have been awful." Annabel touched his shoulder reassuringly. Although meant kindly, somehow Annabel's carefree candour always made him feel worse. Having to 'flee across the world' sounded desperate and dramatic, but he supposed that if he stepped back a bit and looked at their situation objectively, it was.

"Let me know when you're both ready to start work on the vaccine," Pip continued. "I think it sounds like you both need to push on with a positive project. I'm sorry we got sidelined working on the monitor, but I have contacted my uncle who is arranging for you to join him in his lab at St Peter's."

"Yes, that would be brilliant," Lincoln agreed. He found Pip's flashing prosthetic rather at odds with their serious conversation. He tried not to be distracted by it. "We need to push on, not give her too much time to dwell on the past."

"I'll call him now, before I begin my night shift. Oh, and also, would you two like to be added to the rota?" Pip asked.

Lincoln knew he wasn't really asking, as Pip was so laid-back that he didn't issue commands, he ruled by gentle suggestion. Over the last few days, though, Lincoln had gathered that everyone at the Faction here contributed financially one way or another, and until he was working at St Peter's, then it was the easiest way of joining the workforce.

"Yes, please do. It would also be great if we could somehow get a battery pack issued for Deter. I know it's hard with no formal ID, but you might be able to obtain one somehow?" He hoped that the exercise would help keep Deter active and the bar work would force her to be more social. Having her own battery pack to use and add to the house energy bill would also make her feel she was paying her own way. He shook Pip's glowing hand and extricated himself from a mouthful of Annabel's wild hair as she clasped him in a compassionate embrace, then made his way back to his room.

Deter was still fast asleep on his bed, so after dithering about what to do, he eventually carefully climbed onto the bed, settled himself around her and gently pulled the blanket over them both. He thought he wouldn't be able to sleep at all as he wasn't used to sharing his space, but he fell asleep instantly, and in the morning they both woke feeling surprised to see each other there but refreshed and optimistic.

In the early hours, Deter was sort of aware that Lincoln was in bed with her and found his presence hugely comforting. She pulled his arm around her and fell back to sleep as the feeling of being alone slowly began to lift.

They fell into a pattern of sharing a bed. They didn't discuss it; it just became part of their routine and it helped them in their day-to-day life and gave them strength as they began to find their place within the London community.

MARIA AND SELINA

Selina had been to school. It was so exciting! She had been chatting to children during the lunch break and had even climbed over quite a high wall so she could join in their games. She never worried about her mother seeing her there, as she knew Maria was inside in the canteen. This had been going on for quite a few weeks and normally she would race back and get home before Maria, but this time she had fallen badly on the ice and hurt her ankle, so she couldn't climb back out over the wall. The other children immediately took care of her and encouraged her to limp into class with them. Some of the children knew she shouldn't have been there and tried to amalgamate her into their group, but she was spotted by an eagle-eyed teacher who, seeing an injured child, immediately sent her to the medical centre. After they put a tight, blue support bandage on it, they asked her name and tried to find records in order to call someone at home to fetch her. Failing to find any records then set off a relay of concerned nurses and teachers who fruitlessly set about trying to work out which class Selina belonged to and why she wasn't listed anywhere.

Maria arrived and entered the front of the school, looking for the reception. She felt very out of sorts, not only because she couldn't be sure that Selina was there, but also because she had never used the front main entrance before. The school was so familiar but felt upside down. She was used to viewing it from behind the scenes.

Breathlessly, she explained why she was there and was made to wait for a long time while another relay of staff eventually worked out what had happened and linked her to Selina. She was finally shown to the principal's office and treated very kindly as her distress was clear to see. Mr Evans, a large, generous man, made many notes with a ballpoint pen, which he then referred back to when he had pertinent questions. Now that Selina's quarantine was broken, he asked if it was her intention to resume home-schooling or if Maria would like to enrol her at school. He had heard from the nurse that Selina was isolated and craved interaction with her peers, and he was careful to impress this on Maria without making her feel indignant or offended.

No decisions were made, but it was left open for Selina to attend the school if she and Maria wished. Reunited, they both burst into tears, from relief and mixed feelings of contrition and apprehension. Back home they settled into their evening routine, feeling estranged, but whereas Selina fell into remorseful silence, Maria covered up the tension with forced loquaciousness. There was time enough for a serious talk, but for now it was important to refuel, and, throwing caution to the wind, Maria used up both that night's and the next day's rations. They were both keen to avoid the serious conversation they both knew was coming.

Maria rang Andy and tried to keep her voice light, as she knew Selina was listening. Although she was keen that Andy didn't trivialise the situation, she was acutely aware that from his viewpoint it seemed very much a storm in a teacup, as Selina had been one of the points of contention in their brief relationship. Andy found it hard to understand why Maria insisted on keeping Selina in quarantine. There was no knowing how, when or why FED attacked, and it was universally accepted that it was an inevitable part of life. Fighting it was futile and keeping a child apart from the rest of the world was not the guarantee Maria believed it to be and unfair on the child. This didn't, however, stop hundreds of parents from doing the same thing.

"Is your ankle OK? Keep it up on the sofa and after supper I'll give you another dose of pain relief." Maria carefully set a tray down on Selina's lap. "I thought you could do with cheering up, so I've made pigs in blankets to go with our poached eggs." They both looked at their unusually full plates, both knowing that the bacon and sausages were meant for another day. Maria smiled at Selina to show that despite the terrible occurrences of the day, things were OK between them.

"Oh, Mum, I'm so sorry." Selina burst into floods of tears as the tension of the day was released by the demonstration of her mother's love. A big bubble of chastened sorrow had been growing larger and heavier on Selina's shoulders as she realised how worried she had made her mother. She knew she'd done the wrong thing but at the same time she didn't know what else to do, as she was so lonely. She longed to attend school with others her own age and be involved in the complexities that adolescent friendships brought. The comradery, the rivalry, the whispered giggles and secrets, she wanted to be part of it all. She knew contracting FED came with risks, but her mum was fine and managed with a prosthetic leg and at school lots of the children had limbs missing. Everyone knew it was just 'one of those things'. It would be odd to be the only one who was Complete and she'd rather get the disease over with than live in fear of it. It was considered worse if you got it when you were older.

"I was so worried! I didn't think you'd ever do something like that, Selina." Maria lifted her daughter onto her lap. Although she was growing rapidly, she was still small and seeing her daughter cry made Maria want to gather her up and hold her tight.

"I know, I first went out as a sort of dare to myself, you know, just to see if I could, and I only went outside the main door then came back again. The next time I went right round our block, but someone saw me, so I didn't go out for ages after that." Selina felt hot from crying and wanted to move as her mother's embrace was making her even hotter, but she didn't want to spoil the moment.

"I wonder who that was? If they'd known who you were, I'd have expected them to tell me." Maria frowned. She knew most of the residents, although she kept to herself, but as the flat had been her mother's she had known her closest neighbours all her life.

"I don't know. She was old. Anyway, I started looking on the online maps to see where I could go next and what might be interesting to visit. There's nothing much nearby, but then I remembered the school." Selina was warming up to her confession, but she was worried her mum would be so cross. She'd played with the children for a few weeks now and she had laughed with them, run alongside them and, worst of all, touched them. She knew this might make her mum really upset.

"Didn't you worry about me seeing you there?" Maria wiped a tear that was still on Selina's cheek and tucked a stray hair behind her ear.

"I knew you wouldn't, as you never go in the playground at lunchtimes." Realising the true extent of her deception, Selina buried her face in her mother's shoulder as a hot, fresh wave of remorse washed over her, bringing more tears. "I'm so sorry," she wailed. "I knew you'd be so cross, but I was having such fun."

"I know, and that's what you've been missing, isn't it? Fun, with friends your own age. I know how you feel, I truly do, and I'm not cross, just filled with a chilly fear that you'll understand one day when you have children."

"I am sorry, though, for making you worried. I wish I could undo it, but if I do get FED, it's just normal and I want to be normal, like everyone else."

Normal, thought Maria, *what is 'normal' really?* She sighed and turned Selina slightly so she could face her properly.

"Well, it's time for us to reset some ground rules, I think, don't you?"

Selina nodded.

"I am upset for two reasons," Maria began. "One, because you deliberately defied me, knowing all the while how I would feel. That cannot happen again. If you feel so strongly about something, you must come to me first and chat about it. OK?"

Selina nodded again.

"Secondly, the odds of you contracting FED are now quite high and if I had all the money in the world this wouldn't bother me in the slightest, as we could pay for the cure at the first sign of trouble. But we don't have all the money in the world and the new cure they promised isn't created yet."

If only Selina had waited, the new cure might have been free and also without the awful side effects. But if she were carrying the virus, they would just have to face it as best they could.

"How long does it take to show? I mean, if I have it?" Selina said.

"I don't know, to be honest. I think everyone's different. Aren't you scared at all? When I had it, I was not only in pain but really frightened."

"No, the thought of it doesn't worry me. I just want to get it over with."

"But you might never have it if a new cure comes out."

"But that could be years and I don't want to wait years. I want to go to school now. I'm so lonely!" With her outburst Selina started crying again, but this time, instead of turning to her mother for comfort, she turned away, afraid of not being understood.

Maria did understand but had an overview that toughened her resolve. She knew that for Selina, the years stretched out, but for her they raced by, and she knew that in ten years' time Selina would view things very differently, especially if the new cure really was issued and available as promised. As long as Selina could be kept safe for another few years, things would turn out for the best.

"I'm sorry, but you have to trust me. I can't let you out of the apartment until this new cure is issued. It might take years, but it will be worth the wait. You'll be Complete and not only that but able to have children of your own."

She raised her voice as Selina howled with disappointment. She had been hoping that now she had mixed with others she would be allowed to attend school with everyone else. If only she hadn't hurt herself and got caught.

"Listen, Selina, what I will do," Maria continued over the noise, "if you promise to do as you are told and remain here, I will find out if anyone has a kitten we could adopt."

Oh! A kitten! Selina was so surprised; she sat up and stopped wailing to make sure she'd heard correctly.

"A kitten? But you've always said you hate animals and would never have them in the flat."

"I know, but if it stops you feeling lonely, then it's worth it, isn't it? And if we do get one, I don't want to hear any more about school, agreed?"

"Yes, agreed." Selina smiled.

Smit was a small, young tabby with white paws and extra toes. She had arrived all wiry and wary, and had instantly taken refuge under the small dresser in the sitting room, where she swiped playfully at anything Selina dangled within range. She came from the school head cook, who had been so pleased to hand her on as she had made the mistake of taking her back after the first owner had found she didn't want a cat after all. Smit was not happy with her feline mother, as her mother had forgotten who she was, and she and Smit's brother ganged up on her. They leapt confidently out of the cat flap, leaving it to hit Smit in the face as she failed to keep up with them. A fresh wound on her nose accompanied her to her new home as a reminder of her mother's rejection. Selina loved her instantly and passionately, unable to concentrate on anything else. Once she got used to them, Smit became a friendly and loving little cat. Sleeping peacefully most of the time either on or next to Selina but then springing into action demanding food and attention once Maria came through the door after her early morning shift.

Smit sat and watched as the snow continued to fall outside the window, her head twitching with interest, while Selina tried to concentrate on schoolwork. Then they would have a snack together for lunch and Selina would unburden herself about things she wished they were eating or doing instead of being stuck inside six floors up.

On returning from her lunchtime duties, Maria was happy to see that a calm had settled again and that Selina was occupied with Smit, enough, at least, to push school into the background. She bought cheap plastic balls and made a little toy mouse for Selina to dangle from a stick. This kept everyone entertained for hours as they delighted in watching Smit's endeavours to catch her prey.

It was a cold winter and the heat of the summer long forgotten. Those who could afford it chased the sun, leaving those who couldn't to suffer the rigours of harsh conditions in the city and keep the heart of New York beating until spring. As Christmas approached, Maria renewed her campaign to obtain financial support from Ian. A message from their former neighbour, who still kept in touch with both of them, let her know that he and his new wife were taking her children away for the winter to escape the British chill. It was a toss-up between Egypt and South Africa, apparently, as they couldn't decide which would get them more kudos points from their posh private school: the history of apartheid followed by a trip up Table Mountain or a cruise down the Nile to see the ancient pyramids. It was so unfair; fancy holidays with his new family, while his old, cast-off family froze across the other side of the world.

Maria sent an emotional and angry message back to their mutual friend to let him know that she was deeply upset but appreciated him letting her know. She then scrolled down her social media 'Deadbeat Dad' page.

"Fancy summer sun for neglectful father, who leaves his only daughter behind," she typed. "I can't believe you treat your step-children better than your own. Where's the love you promised our child? Oh, no doubt frozen, like your poor little girl's fingers and toes. I don't want anything for myself, just what is owed for our daughter."

She clicked 'post' and the text went live. She coupled it with a photo of Selina in silhouette against the frozen window, drawing little pictures on the misted pane. Selina was actually quite happy at the time, but the picture depicted her seemingly sad and mournful. It instantly had reactions from her friends online, who set off a reel of comments threading down, linking and interlinking in disgust.

"Time that bastard paid."

"Can't believe he'd do this... no, wait, I can. How typical of Ian. Utterly selfish."

"Poor little thing, it's getting really cold here now. Why couldn't he take her with him?"

Maria basked in the attention and fuelled the posts with further emotive comments when her friend's reactions seemed to be slowing down. She hoped that Ian would see her page and be shamed into action. His family were so conscious of their social position in their community they would be sure to want her to shut the page down as soon as possible, and the only way she would do that is if he paid up the maintenance he owed. Selina had been six when they split up, so that was half her life without him; six years' child support owed.

The kitten tried to climb onto her lap and she gently pushed it off. She had an hour to go through Selina's morning task with her, correcting, explaining and then reinforcing, just to make sure. She pulled the notebook over to have a look while Selina took control of the cat. This morning's mathematics in neat columns in front of her, she suddenly felt incredibly sad. Here was her brave little girl, living an isolated life, with just her mother, a cat and her studies to keep her occupied. How different things could have been. If she and Ian had stayed together, they would still be in England, they'd have lovely holidays, Selina could be at school, because her dad would be able to pay for the cure. If need be, she would have comfortable and stylish new prosthetics. No work, none of this juggling three part-time jobs and struggling with basic needs. If only things had been different.

The winter passed slowly and Selina lost the energy to dream of being at school, besides, it was the school holidays now. It was cold, but luckily no one froze inside, as the building relied on geothermal energy to heat the flats and they felt nicely cushioned by their neighbours. So, although it wasn't exactly Crete, it wasn't Siberia either. Ian had chosen the Land of the Pharaohs in the end and had spent Christmas Day in a hotel spa lounging by the pool, making the most of the sun.

Maria had no luck extracting either money or pity from his family and decided that she would try again, taking direct action by writing to his mother. She would wait until the New Year and send pictures and an update as though they hadn't been estranged these past six years. Meanwhile, the snow outside was starting to melt, and no longer glistened enticingly, but began a gradual slide into brown sludge.

"Could you bring me a bit of snow before it all goes?" Selina begged. At the first fall, Maria had indulged Selina by bringing a huge sackful of snow that they filled the sink with, and Selina spent hours playing with it until it eventually disappeared down the plughole.

"Oh, I don't know. It's all dirty now. It's been sitting there for weeks and every cat and dog has turned it slowly yellow."

"Oh, please, Mum. It'll be gone soon."

Maria looked out the window. It was grey and uninviting outside and the light was already falling. She didn't want to go back out there; her stump ached and she just wanted to enjoy the last few days of evenings at home before Andy required her help to sort out sale stock.

"Oh, OK!" She pushed herself up and reluctantly put her warm coat and boots on while Selina excitedly collected a big, old, plastic sack.

"Thank you, Smit and I are so grateful, aren't we, Smit?"

Smit mewed in agreement and rubbed against her legs.

"Right, while I'm gone you need to put the kettle on, I'll need a hot drink when I get back."

"Yes, Mum, we can do that, can't we, Smit?"

Outside the wind whipped menacingly around between the high rises, caught along a concrete tunnel. Maria hugged her arms across her body and scanned the area for the whitest section of snow. The wind turbines were all spinning madly in unison, towering above the old bridge that ran over the road carrying an outdated railway line, and high above the bridge arched the tracks for the bugs taking people into the city. The centre of Manhattan was a protected heritage site, so no new tracks were allowed, but the bugs ran freely everywhere else. They were expensive, though. Each small vessel had enough room for four people to sit and travel in, and they ran regularly throughout the day and night. Anyone wanting to transport more than four people could commandeer the community bus, which was also powered by electricity, which the user had to pay for in fuel cells from their own store at home. Most wealthy people had their own vehicles, though, which Maria looked at jealously from her usual seat on the public bus.

Luckily, no one had travelled, except by foot, and the ground was only disturbed by endless layers of footprints, including her own. An almost-pristine area at the base of the bridge looked quite deep and the best place to begin. Maria heaped huge handfuls into the sack, only stopping when it was finally full and almost too heavy to lift. She carefully hoisted it over her shoulder and started towards the door.

"Goodness, isn't there enough of it outside, do you really need to bring it inside too?" A gently teasing male voice made her stop, and she turned to see a kind, elderly gentleman holding the door open for her.

"Well, seeing as I'm the Ice Queen, how else will I stay so young and beautiful?"

"Ah, witty as well as modest!" He smiled as she stepped into the lift. "Well, better make the most of it, they'll be bringing the snow ploughs in soon to take it all away."

"Yes, let's hope they manage to collect it all before it melts and causes major floods like the last time."

"I know! You'd think they'd have it organised by now." He held the door open for her as they both headed for the lifts. "Which floor, your majesty?" he asked, poised to press the lift buttons.

She smiled. "The sixth, please."

"Ah, well my sixth sense is telling me you're in for a disappointing time. That will have melted by morning."

"My daughter is under quarantine but is desperate to play with it before it all goes." She could see a puddle on the floor of the lift was pooling under the sack. "Oh dear, it's making rather a mess already."

"Don't you worry! I'll mop it up. I hope you have fun while it lasts."

"Thank you so much, that's so kind."

The door opened on the sixth floor and she left the old man as he continued upwards, while she struggled to the door of her flat.

The snow didn't look nearly as appealing as last time, but Selina was very happy and played contentedly until bedtime making mini snow sculptures and building a whole snow town, including a pond with mini ducks for Smit to watch. Maria found it hard to sleep, partly as, being on holiday, she wasn't falling into her bed exhausted after a day's work, but also because she was feeling restless, brought on by the imminent New Year. She often considered a change of job at this time of year, resolving to find something that challenged her a little more and offered progression. The problem was that there was never time to actively look for something. Also, she doubted anyone would want her, as she had been stuck in her school jobs for the past five years. She'd been slim and glamorous once, but now all that was left was her crowning glory, her luxurious waves of thick, dark hair.

She sat up, looking through her social media feed and an article caught her eye. "Who are we? What is 'normal'?"

It interested her, as it was something Selina had said that she so desperately wanted to be. By definition, 'normal' means conforming to the standard or the common type: usual, not abnormal, regular, natural. Selina wanted FED so that she could be the same and hang out with other kids, talking about prosthetics, mixing up skin colours, adding colour and lights and being able to rotate their hands and feet 360 degrees. There was pain and discomfort, but that was managed, and the fashion was to make your new limbs part of your identity.

Maria understood that Selina felt she was excluded from something that young people felt was cool, but from an adult perspective, the risks were so high. Many children lost function of their organs, as well as their limbs, and the disease was unpredictable and indiscriminate. Some people had very little flesh lost afterwards, a nibbling of an ear or a toe, maybe, but others lost their lives. It was rare, but it still happened. The thought of losing her one and only beloved child filled Maria with such terror, but how could she stop time?

If only they had greater resources and could afford the cure. She looked up 'get rich quick', but it soon became clear there was no such thing. Smart shopping and utilising unwanted items was something she already did, and she had no interest in signing up for something that deliberately kept details of the actual job secret. Then she saw an advert for human hair. She clicked on a price calculator and entered her details. Hers was long, nearly twenty-four inches to her waist and was un-dyed, dark, thick Mexican hair. The calculator valued her hair at a ridiculous amount: nearly a whole month's combined wage. This started her off on a trail searching to see what else people were looking for. It seemed almost everything was for sale. Hands were more popular than legs and while it was listed under 'donors wanted', there were discretionary 'expenses' that could be received. She had never thought of selling her arms before, but there was no reason why not. The 'expenses' more than covered the cost of brand-new prosthetic limbs and compensated for any associated problems with the amputation. She was glad her arms were still intact and wondered if the amount would cover a new leg too.

She totted up the amount she could potentially make by donating both arms and her hair, and then set it against the current cost of the cure. Incredibly, it would pay for half the dose that Selina would need. If she could get Ian to promise to pay the other half, then she would consider lifting the quarantine. Her head filled with desperate and irrational ideas, she finally headed for the bathroom, where the snow town in the bathtub was subsiding. Amused and touched by the once carefully crafted details, she smiled as she finally headed for bed.

In the cold light of day, her scheme didn't seem quite such a good idea. Maria watched her hands complete their day-to-day tasks so quickly, efficiently and painlessly. It would be pretty tricky learning to live without them. Besides, it was only two more years until the new vaccine came out.

She finished her morning shift, which was mainly spent listening to Bonny giving her a gossipy news update covering everything from the headmaster's new assembly times (deliberately trying to upset the cleaning staff's timetable) to the rumour that the Complete Immune had been seen in London.

"How would she have got over there? Can't be her, if you ask me. I reckon they all blew up in the explosion that took out the Faction's headquarters. No one could have survived that. Did you see the pictures?"

Maria nodded, although to be honest, she couldn't remember seeing any.

"That's it, all over for the Faction. They've gone so quiet. That's what happens, though, isn't it, if your leaders are gone? Look at the history department! You wouldn't know this school had one without Mr Armitage. He used to do wonderful displays in the corridor, great, big timelines stretching right back, every child's face featuring as key characters. My Ben was so proud to be Walt Disney! And now look at the state of it." She gestured to the clean, empty walls. These were actually a conscious decision by the current head, who felt a tidy wall reflected a well-ordered educational establishment.

Maria sighed, sensing that Bonny hadn't finished her tirade yet, but Bonny took her sigh as agreement over the sorry state of the empty hallways. "Without Mr Armitage, his department is leaderless, yes, leaderless, and the same is true of the Faction. Anyway, I'm sure everything will settle down now, won't it? We have to trust, don't we? Trust that the Establishment knows what's best."

Maria was distracted by Bonny's hands, which kept up a constant twittering, much like her mouth, and she realised that Bonny's left hand was a particularly realistic prosthetic. All these years she'd worked alongside her and never stopped to think or question which of her limbs were real. It was as Selina said, totally normal. She supposed everyone knew she had only one leg as she definitely limped, but if she found a painless new prosthetic, her limp would probably be gone. What an ironic situation, to emulate being Complete but to consider such a state as an oddity.

Back at home, the cat started stalking around her, demanding breakfast as soon as she got in the door. Selina was still in bed and so Maria started cooking so she could wake Selina to the smell of toast.

A modest array of condiments, including honey from the housing block bees, some cream cheese on the turn and the usual jams, were laid out ready for them both. The cat crunched on her biscuits, managing to eat and purr at the same time, while arching her back, asking to be stroked. Pausing to enjoy her cup of tea in the quiet solitude, she looked out into the street below. Someone must have a trip planned, as the community bus was idling in the layby, but apart from that it was quiet, just the usual comings and goings as most people left for work or school. She turned her thoughts to the morning home-schooling and wondered whether it would be best to look at natural resources or the history of transport as a topic today.

"Selina?" She turned, calling, trying to make her soft voice louder by aiming it directly at Selina's door. "Sweetheart, it's time to get up. Smit has had her breakfast; it's time for yours. If you take too long your toast will go soggy."

She went and stood in the door, turned the light on and then opened the curtains. Turning the light back off, she sat on the bed and prised the covers from Selina's face. Something wasn't right. Selina was deeply unresponsive. Maria checked she was still breathing and then felt her forehead. It was burning up. She knew the signs all too well and checked all over Selina's body. There were red swellings on her feet, but nowhere else yet. If she were lucky, they would stay just on her feet, like Maria's had.

It was definitely FED and even though she had been preparing for this, it still came as a shock, and Maria felt an icy fear grip her tightly around her chest.

She rang the hospital and within ten minutes, the emergency services arrived. Two nurses, kind, firm and efficient, gently explained that Selina would be requiring around-the-clock care until the fever broke and the red swellings turned from ugly abscesses to black scabs. Would she like to pay for the cure now to halt the damage? If not, did she have a healthcare plan? If not, then medical bills would be issued weekly. The cure, of course, was optional but even without it, medical bills would be crippling. If cash payments were not forthcoming, then they would be forced to take a look at both her liquid and fixed assets. They took a good look around, sizing up her belongings and asked to see proof of ownership of the property. She knew that if they didn't like what they saw then Selina would be left at home. There was no way she could risk Selina's life, so hospital was the only option.

Folding up her title deeds, she carefully put them back into her small safe alongside their passports, birth certificates and her divorce papers. While the nurses transferred Selina to a gurney, setting up various intravenous feeds to ensure Selina remained hydrated and to boost her immune system, Maria tried to pack essentials. She tried to think clearly, but she felt paralysed by uncertainty and ended up over-packing, which meant the huge, heavy overnight bag, added pressure to the weight of worry that already ground her down.

She meekly signed all paperwork without really looking, then followed as the gurney left the flat, descended in the lift and then made a swift, uninterrupted journey by ambulance to the hospital.

ANGUS

The shelter he had made from the remains of the bomb shelter, buttressed by tightly packed snow, was starting to melt, leaving slushy puddles and hollow promises echoing through the wreckage.

Clicking impatiently at the puppy to follow, Angus led the way through the streets, looking for answers. He knew that every day someone fell victim to FED, someone who couldn't afford the cure or lengthy stays in hospital. Battling infections and going through rehabilitation on your own was hard and most people didn't make it. He needed to find a new team and new family so he could resume his fight for justice.

He cut through streets concisely until he reached the river crossing into Brooklyn. The further south he went, the more impoverished it became. This was somewhere Deter and her friends never set foot. The wealthy few in Manhattan lived as though no flesh-eating disease could or would ever interrupt their shopping schedule. On the other side, it was an unhealthy dose of reality.

In between the empty and dilapidated streets were small communities. They didn't have much, but what they had they shared. They also knew exactly who needed help and who was beyond help. Those beyond it often saw their possessions walking out the door into their neighbour's house before they even drew their last breath, but that didn't surprise them, as everyone knew the rules. Angus was looking, searching for God's sign as he strode through Crown Heights into Brownsville.

No one watching Angus would think to stop him or challenge him, even the most aggressively territorial recognised the damage his arsenal of weapons could do. His sense of purpose gave him courage, but he knew he was watched and tracked as he made his way into a deserted tower block. Set apart from the other buildings, this one, although run down, had the air of being inhabited. There were no obvious security measures, so he walked right in. He found himself in a wide, empty reception area. He looked at the remaining furnishings, an incongruous mix of broken desks and several large beds, one with no mattress or bedding but a row of children's toys placed carefully lined up along the top. The other bed was made up to showroom standard, with a fluffy pillow left plump and inviting. He sat down on it, instantly spoiling the arrangement and sinking into the unexpected luxury of a warm, soft resting place. He closed his eyes to enjoy the unwinding of his tense and rigid muscles.

He and the puppy woke after a deep but short sleep. He felt he'd literally only just shut his eyes.

Someone was shaking him. "You can't sleep here, it isn't right," a voice hissed. The voice was deep, low, female, edged with fear but with more than an ounce of determination.

"Wake up, soldier. Quick! Before Aline comes." The insistent nagging was coupled with quite painful pinching on his ears and eyebrows, dragging him into consciousness.

Opening his eyes, he saw a row of concerned faces, who all then started talking at once, to both him and each other.

"Who are you?"

"Lucky you woke up."

"What are you doing here?"

"He can't stay!"

"Well, what we gonna do? Get up, get up!" The pinching continued until he stood up and then they began slapping him and pushing him towards the door.

"Wait!" he bellowed, taking a step back. "I was brought here for a purpose."

"Whatever your purpose, we don't need it, so keep moving." The hands started pushing again. The woman who had woken him was short and very plump and only came up to his chest, but she had her finger pointed at him and she was waving it like she could spin him round and round on the end of it.

"We don't like it when people march in and just lay down on our beds! What would Aline say? Huh? You can turn around and march right back out and keep soldiering on, soldier boy!"

"That's right, Margaret, you tell him. He has no right to be here."

"Aline won't be happy."

"Anyone seen Aline?"

"What's she gonna say?"

"Disgraceful."

Angus stood still as they continued trying to push him out the door. He felt a sudden calm and clarity, and, still keeping his eyes closed, he began to sing. It was an old song. One he had sang in worship all his life. It came to him out of nowhere, but it swept through him like a powerful force and he had no choice but to open his mouth and sing:

"Amazing grace, how sweet the sound.
That saved a wretch like me.
I once was lost, but now I'm found.
Was blind but now I see."

His voice deep and soulful, his grief was released for a few moments as the melody poured out of him.

Around him a surprised silence and then as he paused for breath, voices took over singing the next phrase.

"'Twas grace that taught, my heart to fear.
And grace, my fears relieved.
How precious did that grace appear,
The hour I first believed.
Through many dangers, toils and snares,
I have already come.
'Tis grace that brought me safe thus far,
And grace will lead us home."

Suspended in the moment, it took a while for Angus to open his eyes, but when he did it was to see warm, kind faces, equally moved by the devotional hymn.

This time a gentle hand reached out and led him outside and then along to a hall that was used for large gatherings. At first quiet and respectfully silent, they soon began chattering again. He gathered that Aline was on her way and that people were bringing refreshments; it seemed the hymn had opened a doorway into their community and had now prompted some kind of party.

Pausing on the threshold, he was ushered through the increasingly noisy and busy room, which filled with more and more people, now dancing and moving to an impromptu band made of anything and everything that rattled and clanged.

Delicious, simple, homemade dishes arrived and were laid out on a long table, and the room was filled with a sense of celebration.

It seemed he had triggered something important, but he didn't know what. Swaying with the insistent rhythm that permeated the room, he took the food and drink he was offered and allowed himself to be steered towards the back of the room, where people were starting to gather and could chat as it was furthest from the music. He sat by a young man with bright neon yellow and silver prosthetic arms and no legs at all, but he was fixed onto a homemade seat with wheels that brought him up to table height. The seat was also painted a vivid yellow and Angus nearly tripped over the wheels, as he didn't see them under the table.

"I'm Barney." Smiling, the young man offered Angus a silver hand.

"Angus."

"Everyone's been waiting and hoping you'd arrive."

"How do you know who I am?" Angus said.

"We don't. But Aline's been waiting for someone to come and show us the way and when you started singing, we knew."

"Knew what."

"That you'd arrived, of course!"

Angus smiled. He had felt it too, a strong and indescribable connection to this community. He had trusted Him and now He had brought him here. He closed his eyes in prayer.

"Amen."

"Amen," Barney echoed reverently.

Some things you don't question. Some things you just accept, and Angus opened up his grief-stricken and traumatised being to the new possibilities these people offered wholeheartedly. He felt hope. Here was the new army he had been looking for, but these soldiers would not bear arms. This army would be fighting in God's name for a new and better world. War had been the Faction's undoing; they had thought they could defeat the Establishment, but they should have kept their cool and remained the angry underdog, snapping at their heels. Thinking of dogs, he was reminded of his own. His loyal companion, who he hadn't wanted or asked for but had grown remarkably fond of. He could feel the puppy under the table, lying almost on top of his feet. It was comforting knowing he was there. He dropped a couple of scraps from his plate on the floor and listened as Barney chattered cheerfully next to him.

At six foot five, Aline towered over most of the others and Angus could see her as she moved across the room. He knew it must be her, partly by the way everyone else moved respectfully aside as she passed, but also by the focussed and purposeful way she looked about the room. Greeting everyone around her, but with a cool reserve and detachment, she strode pretty much directly towards him.

Once she reached him, she faltered slightly, as though suddenly unsure, and she opened her mouth to speak but seemed undecided about how to begin.

"Aline, take my space at the table." Barney quickly wheeled out the way and someone else hastily bought a chair.

She sat down and the room seemed to exhale. Gentle chatter soon bubbled up around them again. She cleared her throat. "Welcome to Brownsville. Have you been this far south before?"

"Thank you," said Angus. "No, this is the first time I've come across the river."

"What brought you to us?" Aline stared at him intently.

"I felt drawn here. It's hard to say by what exactly. But I felt guided here, by our good lord." Aline nodded as though she already knew, so he continued, "I could sense I was being watched, but I didn't feel threatened and I found a big room with an odd assortment of furniture and in the middle there was a bed."

"You saw the bed?" Aline asked sharply.

"I did. It looked so inviting, I lay down on it," Angus said.

Aline flinched. "We don't lie down in that bed. Not unless…" She hesitated and then said with finality, "It's been kept sacred for many, many years."

"Oh?" Angus was curious, as he'd wondered earlier what the issue was with the bed.

Evading his curiosity, she continued, "But I knew you were coming. I have been feeling it for many weeks. We have been praying for change and now He has answered. What that change will be is yet to be seen, but for now let's rejoice in His benevolence." She raised a glass. "Peace and hope."

"To peace and hope." Angus lifted his glass to touch hers.

He sat back, reflecting on the past few months, the futile loneliness of his vigil by the wreckage of the Faction's headquarters. His hunger and thirst, for not just physical nourishment, but for his spirit and soul, had become almost too much to bear. Sustained only by his faith, he was grateful and relieved that his trust in Him had been rewarded.

There were no concrete answers or solid plans yet, but these people felt like a much welcome new family and the way they had embraced him led him to believe that they felt the same way about him.

MARIA AND SELINA

"Mum, I'm so thirsty, my mouth feels funny," Selina croaked, as she came around after days of being unconscious. She still had a fever and had been vomiting, although there was very little left in her stomach to bring up. The doctor had recommended regular blood transfusions and intravenous antibiotic therapy, as the sores on her legs started to turn into huge blisters covering the whole of her lower legs from the knee downward. Maria anxiously scanned the latest medical bill.

"Sweetheart, you are doing so well. The worst is over and it looks like it's only your legs that have been affected, which is brilliant news."

"Oh, good! Can I have legs like Carol Archer?"

Carol Archer was an incredible athlete with powerful, high-impact prosthetics that gleamed sleekly as she ran. She started off as a sprinter who gained popularity not just because she won most of her races but also because she was incredibly beautiful. She had many fans, but particularly young girls, who followed her every fashion move, from her latest haircut to her cutting-edge sprint feet. She only wore realistic feet for red carpet events as it was important to be seen in the latest heels, but most of the time she was modelling or trialling the latest performance limbs. Selina loved the idea of being Carol, to be running outside, fast and strong. She had been longing to experience this freedom herself for years now. The pain in her legs felt like they were on fire and to be honest, they were a bit smelly, which wasn't very nice, but that didn't matter as she was so excited by the prospect of finally being able to go to school and do normal things like go the shops.

"We'll see!" Maria smiled. "Meanwhile, you've got to rest, so try and sleep as much as you can."

"Yes, Mummy."

As Selina drifted off, dreaming of new legs and new friends, Maria tried to organise her finances. She had no savings, as they lived hand to mouth, and there had been no response from the messages she had sent Ian.

This week's wages would only cover a tiny percentage of this week's medical bill, so she would have to either find a better job or look into alternative ways to raise funds. She looked up the details of the buyer for natural hair and sent them a quick message. No commitment, just an enquiry, and she attached a picture of her hair in case.

Almost immediately a message pinged back in return:

"Maria,

Thank you for your enquiry, we'd be really interested to meet you to give you a more accurate price for your hair. Hair must be uncoloured and without heat damage or split ends.

Prices are based on lengths and depend on quality.
Minimum length fourteen to fifteen inches
Medium length sixteen to eighteen inches
Premium length nineteen inches and above.

Should you be unable to visit your nearest salon then please secure your hair in a tight ponytail before cutting. No loose hair will be accepted."

She looked at Selina sleeping peacefully and checked the time. She had a few hours before she was due at Andy's, so she checked the location of the salon and left the hospital.

Sitting in the bus looking out, as traffic started building up, she checked the time impatiently. She felt tempted to get out and walk as an elderly lady wobbling past on a pushbike overtook the bus. She sighed. In many ways not having control over the journey was a blessing; there was nothing to be done except wait.

There were still several daylight hours left, so where were all these people on the roads heading? New Yorkers lived much as they always had, with their refusal to compromise on luxury, unimpeded by their modern-day disabilities. Despite the surrounding walls that kept the dangers of the elements at bay, there was a decay threatening the preserved fragment of the superpower that it still claimed to be. Travelling alone in the bus with only her thoughts and fears for company, Maria felt the insipient change in the wind, mirrored by her own shift in priorities. She would not live with debt and she would not live without having given Selina the absolute best medical care. That meant that, whatever happened, she had to provide income to cover the bills, and she would do it any way possible. She would stop expecting Ian to contribute and start finding solutions herself.

The bus stopped outside a remarkably smart shop selling kitchenware, which she would usually have been easily distracted by, but after consulting her map she tracked the hair salon five doors down. The salon had a gloriously ostentatious front with fractured mirrors creating a mosaic tribute to ancient Greece with scantily clad damsels wrapped around pillars beckoning you in. Inside, six chairs in front of well-lit, flattering mirrors (decorated in a similar style to the entrance) dominated the room, but only two stylists were working that day. One was mid-haircut, working on a plump, middle-aged woman with very limp, thin hair. The stylist was working exceedingly hard to inject volume into it, but the woman wasn't taking much notice as she was glued to a programme on a portable device. Maria tried to catch the eye of the stylist, but he refused to look up; he was too intent on his task. In the corner a very slim, young girl was mixing something in a dish while her client, an equally young lady, chatted about some film they had both seen. Maria hadn't been to see a film for years and only really watched things Selina enjoyed so had no idea what they were talking about. She smiled at the stylist, who smiled back but made no effort to find out if she needed help.

Not knowing quite what to do next, Maria looked at the reception desk to see if there was a bell to ring. No bell, but there was a beautifully handwritten sign:

"Hair appointments? Please wait,
Sorry if we're running late.
Take the weight off your feet
And help yourself to a sweet.
If you're here to sell your wares,
Turn left, then up the stairs."

The stylists still didn't pay her any attention, so she helped herself to one of the mints in a bowl and followed instructions by taking the stairs.

Marcus Ward had once been an attractive man with thick, glossy locks to advertise his skills in the hairdressing trade. He still coloured it an optimistic shade of palomino, but it no longer suited his ageing skin. He pranced up to Maria, almost neighing with delight as he grasped her long, dark hair in his clammy hands. He shot her what he thought was a seductive glance and held it up to the light.

"Oh, my dear lady, the condition is delightful, such a rarity!" he whinnied. "Almost everyone has coloured their hair at one time or another, but yours is genuinely virginal."

His emphasis on the word 'virginal' was slightly unpleasant, so Maria replied tartly, "I've never seen the point of colouring it, you only have to keep it up once you start and it's an extra cost that I simply can't afford." Maria tried to politely shake her hair out of his grasp, but he wasn't letting go.

"At least twenty inches, I should think."

"It's twenty-four, but as you don't pay more for over nineteen inches, then nineteen is all I will sell."

"Oh, we can negotiate, dear lady, we can negotiate. After all, you must be keen to make a sale as you have arrived on my doorstep only..." He looked at his watch. "Well... thirty-five minutes after my message."

Maria hesitated.

"Take a seat." Marcus trotted over to an old-fashioned barber's chair. He smiled encouragingly and Maria had an image flash through her mind of the demon barber of Fleet Street.

He measured and haggled, and she sat tall and unyielding until they agreed on her original price, which was just over a month's combined wages. This would pay off her medical bills to date and cover the next few weeks at least. With Selina in recovery, then it wouldn't be long before she could be discharged. With luck they could be home by next week, leaving them with a small pot of money to put by for later.

They agreed he could have the lot, so she watched with very mixed feelings as he carefully combed her hair, then divided it into tiny bunches. Around these tiny bunches he fixed extremely tight bands. Using a combination of small, sharp scissors and a blade, he cut and shaved above each ponytail, harvesting the maximum of her tresses, until all that was left was a raggedy, ugly mess.

As he worked, she found herself telling him about Selina and why she was forced to sell her hair; she didn't know why she felt she had to confide in this odious man, but she didn't want him to think badly of her. As he worked, she talked and somehow couldn't stop. When he finished, she didn't recognise herself. Seeing herself like this, she wanted to burst into tears but, already embarrassed by feeling she'd shared too many confidences, she pushed the feeling down until it formed a hard, cold lump in her stomach. After he had admired the neat pile of hair laid out on his desk, Marcus lathered her head as if it was a client's stubbly beard and efficiently shaved off everything that was left.

"You must come back," he said. "As soon as you have more than fourteen inches, we'd be delighted to do business with you again."

"I hope I never have to do that again," she replied; her head felt weird and vulnerable. "This will be enough money to see Selina and I through."

"Well, if you change your mind, here, take my card." He handed her a card that said 'Sanctum'. "Plus, if there's anything else you ever want to donate, let me know." He winked knowingly.

"What's that supposed to mean? I thought you were a hairdresser?"

"I am… so if someone needs a wig, I help them find the right hair… but… also… if they need a replacement limb, I can help them find that too."

She frowned. "I had heard that people sometimes paid for donor limbs, but it's not entirely legal is it?"

"It's not exactly illegal either," Marcus said. "Anyone can be a donor, for blood, organs, tissue. It's just that sometimes, if someone needs something specific, and they're prepared to pay, well, then, for the right price, I can help them jump the queue."

"I did see something about this on the Internet, but…" She paused, unsure if she trusted him and disgusted that she was even thinking about it.

"Oh, it's all done properly," he reassured her, tossing his bleached mane casually as he turned on a huge screen, which he angled to her viewpoint. "This is an amazing clinic, and I mean *amazing*. It has the most beautifully designed interior and exterior, with gorgeous views for every patient. Both recipient and donor have similar rooms and it's your choice if you wish to meet."

"It's on a ship!" Maria exclaimed as the photographs showed sea views from the suites.

"Yes, a truly deluxe luxury liner! Do take my card and look us up… all details should you wish to be a donor, or even a scout."

"A scout?" said Maria.

"Yes! Now why didn't I think of that before? It would be the perfect career for you! It would help you find that bit extra to pay for your daughter's medical care. As a scout, you'd be earning a huge commission for finding donors for us." Marcus twiddled his hair.

"I don't think so, really." Maria looked at her watch; she'd be late for Andy. "I must go, but thank you anyway."

She carefully placed the cash he gave her in a zipped compartment in her bag and shoved the business card next to it.

As she left, she caught a glimpse of a plump, bald, Latino girl in the huge mirrors and didn't recognise herself. Outside, she wished she had a hat or scarf, as the slightest breeze reminded her of her lack of hair. She wasn't looking forward to seeing Andy; he would be shocked by her new look, but what else was she supposed to do?

At the hospital, two specialists crowded around Selina as the nurses tried to cool her down with spray bottles.

She had been stripped of covers; she had ice packs draped over her and had been moved to a bed with a cooling mattress. Maria was asked to move to one side while they tried to get her temperature down.

"Nothing to worry about." The nurse patted her reassuringly. "Fevers always seem worse than they are. It's just the body trying to get rid of the infection. What the doctor is concerned about, though, is why Selina is having a relapse and whether it's linked to FED or not."

"She was fine yesterday, I don't know what's going on!" Maria was frantic.

"Not to worry, it's just a fever. I'd go and get a coffee if I were you while she gets over the worst."

But it wasn't fine. Selina remained unconscious for two days while large, bruise-like marks spread up her legs and over her hands. The doctors were interested to hear she had spent her life in quarantine and privately wondered if this might have contributed to the relapse. They prepared to operate to remove the infected areas as quickly as possible and drew up the incision points with thick, black markers. They would have to remove both arms just above the elbow and both legs. One would be just above the knee, but the other right up to her hip. It was a simple and relatively uncomplicated procedure as luckily no internal organs were affected. That's when it got tricky.

Selina's immune system was not robust and it was unclear if she would survive. Post-operative infection was a risk, and so was haemorrhaging and the spread of FED, so regular exposure to ultraviolet light would be recommended, as well as high doses of specialist antibiotics. As the doctors' orders totted up, so did the list of costs, and that didn't even include the rehabilitation service and prosthetics. Maria's fund from the sale of her hair wasn't going to have as much impact on her debts as she'd hoped. The hospital aimed to get most healthy children on a two-week turnaround with physical and emotional therapy starting immediately. After two months, the patient was expected to be completing basic tasks, returning to school or work and using their new limbs confidently. It didn't look as though Selina would be leaving for at least another two weeks and she'd already been with them seven days. To compound the hopelessness of their finances, Maria's ability to work grew to a halt as she couldn't concentrate on anything and she didn't want to spend a minute away from Selina.

After her third day at the hospital, sleeping on the floor next to Selina's bed, Andy called round. He found her inspecting Selina's stumps that were just starting to heal nicely and as soon as Maria caught sight of his kind, familiar face, she began sobbing. Weeks of stress poured out with her tears into his sympathetic arms and she was left feeling exhausted. As he comforted her, Andy still couldn't get used to her shaved head, but it gave her a softness and exposed her vulnerability, which made him feel protective and reminded him of what he'd first found attractive about her. He'd thought her hair had been the most beautiful thing about her, but without it, he could see her strength and sacrifice was far more alluring.

He bought her food and drink and clean clothes, which he'd found more complicated to buy than he'd anticipated and then, as Selina continued sleeping, he took Maria to his flat and put her to bed where she slept for twenty hours without stirring. On waking they called the hospital, but as there was no change, he insisted that they go for breakfast and a walk in the park. The fresh air was a welcome cleanser for her mind and soul. Maria started to put things in perspective and began planning for Selina's return. Although the money from her hair had been swallowed up, she would find a way to raise the finances. The spring sun was starting to warm up the earth and the world was whispering its creative secrets as new life began to stir. When Andy offered her his hand, Maria took it, even though she knew he was offering more than just friendship. Why not? She thought, *We have always been friends even when the relationship broke down. We never stopped liking each other; maybe we can make it work this time?*

"I've looked into these amazing children's neuro-prosthetics, they come from Finland and are really popular at the moment. The kids call them 'props' and they are such cool colours. Or the doctors say that if we can afford it, then transplants might be an option. They aren't a hundred per cent sure that she'll cope with major surgery yet, but in a few years, who knows?"

Maria ran her fingers over her head. It would be years before her hair reached a decent length. "Both sound amazing! But there's no rush, is there? I expect Selina will have plenty of ideas of her own. The prosthetics sound cool and an affordable option and just what she has been looking forward to. We have lots of time to research them properly." Maria smiled at his use of the word 'we' and felt a huge weight lift as she finally felt she could share her burdens. "What went wrong with us?" said Maria as Andy pulled her in closer.

"Oh, that'll be my jealousy over your love for Selina and your stubbornness and fierce sense of independence!"

Maria playfully pushed Andy, giving him a gentle pinch in the ribs. "OK, no need for such brutal honesty, but I'm glad we can talk about it." Maria looked up searchingly into his eyes. "How do we know things will be different this time?"

"We don't." He kissed her on the temple where she used to have cute, wispy curls. "We just take each day as it comes and try and remind ourselves to do better this time."

"Sounds good, I'm willing to try and do better." She linked arms as they took the path back towards Andy's flat. They passed the pond and an old man who was feeding the ducks. It made her realise that life went on. People were ill and dying, but here was a man enjoying the simple pleasure of sharing his bread with local wildlife. The juxtaposition gave her added resolve.

She felt strong as she returned to the hospital, and even when Selina cried, saying something heavy was crushing her feet, Maria felt that she could cope. The phantom pain would pass and soon Selina would be just like every other child, and happy to be 'normal'.

"Just think of finally being able to go to school, think of all the new friends you're going to make," she whispered.

Selina was overjoyed to come home but distraught to find that Smit wasn't there. She was expecting her welcoming cries as they came through the door.

"She always rushes to see you when you've been at work, I've always wanted her to rush to see me," Selina cried. "Where can Smit be?"

"I don't know what happened, darling, but she's not in the flat so she must have found a new home." Maria couldn't believe she'd forgotten about the cat! She had left in such a hurry and hadn't actually returned until a few days ago as Andy had been insistent that she shouldn't be alone. It was only when she came to prepare the flat for Selina's homecoming that she remembered. Who knew where Smit was? She must have slipped out as they left. Luckily, Selina was so excited by choosing her 'props' she was easily distracted. Plus, they had little jaunts to the shops to look forward to, not to mention enrolling at the school.

"One thing at a time," she said firmly as she kissed her daughter goodnight.

Selina had to put up with four weeks in a wheelchair and then when her props arrived, she would be back in for surgery to have her implants fitted. These connected with her nerves so that she would be able to control the prosthetics using her brain. Maria's were a less sophisticated version and needed updating badly, but Selina's needs came first. The flat was now mortgaged to help cover costs and, unknown to Selina, Maria had sold the Monopoly set and a few other heirlooms and jewellery from her marriage to Ian. She had always vowed that she would never part with these things but needs must. There would still be a shortfall, but Maria had a plan and felt in control, and that now the worst had happened they could only move onward and upwards.

"You will bring her in immediately if she comes home, won't you, Mummy?"

"Yes, of course, even if you're fast asleep I'll bring her in to see you." Maria watched as Selina arranged her covers over her short stumps and contentedly closed her eyes.

Now… if only they could find that bloody cat!

At 5pm on a cold Tuesday in January, Maria found herself outside Marcus Ward's ostentatious establishment yet again. The mirrored pillars were still there, as were the flirtatious nymphs, but the interior was now a rich, opulent purple with the stylists dressed in gold. This time Marcus was in the salon and he spotted her before she had time to change her mind and leave. He trotted over and pulled the door open with a flourish, calling loudly to her in greeting. "Mariiaaa! I have been hoping you'd revisit us. How charming you look, what a sexy little pixie you make with your elfin hair."

Flattered he remembered her, but also anxious that he might be indiscreet about her visit, she hovered in the doorway. "Could I have a chat… upstairs?" she asked.

"Of course, we were just finishing for the day down here. Justin, Amy, could you be sweeties and clear away? Don't forget the sign on the door and lock up after you."

Marcus swept upstairs, trailing a powerful eau de cologne, and ushered her into his office. Nothing had changed upstairs, and she sat on the chair opposite his and wondered how to begin.

"I have been thinking, about our last conversation," she said. "It's not an easy decision, but on your website everything seems quite simple. I find willing donors for hair, limbs and organs, and then bring them to meet you and once they sign up I get paid. Is that right?"

"Completely! Excuse the pun! It's so simple, and I do all the boring bits, negotiating and paperwork – you just make the introductions. We are a highly regarded company and it's all above board. Business is growing at a rapid rate, so we would be overjoyed to add you to our blossoming team." Marcus flashed her a dazzling smile. "The elite few can afford to ditch the prosthetics and finally wake up in full control of their own bodies. No maintenance, no recharging, no upgrading necessary, no discomfort. I know the younger generation are interested in high-spec stuff with a penchant for all-singing, all-dancing 'props', but there's many who'll pay for a simple life, just natural skin and bone, and the ability to truly feel every sensation. Who doesn't miss that?"

"Well, I can feel things quite well."

"But not perfectly," Marcus interrupted. "Nothing is as perfectly made as our own flesh and blood. Or someone else's," he added.

"To be honest, I can't remember. I lost my leg a long time ago."

"Well, one of the perks of working for us is that you can take advantage of our exclusive members offers. I took advantage, not once, not twice, but three times." He lifted each leg and then raised his left hand to show her a neat, white line above his wrist.

"Both legs brand new, one above the knee, one below and a hand transplant. Look at the size of that scar tissue, you can hardly see it! Amazing match, very similar gene pool. I walk with a spring in my step, as I feel Complete!"

"What about if I didn't want the members perks for myself, could I transfer the offer to someone else?" Maria said.

"By someone else, I assume you mean your daughter?"

"Yes." There was no point in pretending otherwise.

"Well, to be honest, I'm not sure, we'd have to ask. But I don't see why not."

Maria felt elated. She could finally see a positive future for Selina and herself. Her new job would provide income and opportunities beyond anything she'd ever imagined, and although there was still a slight nagging doubt about the ethics behind the business, she refused to let her conscience bring her down. She would discuss the job with Andy, but not yet, she wanted to have a clear plan in mind to prove to him that she knew what she was doing. Meanwhile, she would continue cleaning and catering at the school, and when Selina was recovered and was at school full-time, then she'd start recruiting donors. She had nothing to lose; all she would be doing was introducing people to Marcus and it was up to him to do the rest. After all, she'd profit, and she knew her friends like Bonny would jump at the chance to make a bit of cash too. It was entirely their choice what they then decided to donate; she would just be providing the opportunity.

Back home she spread out Selina's stationery and began planning her first steps. Her initial priority would be building contacts, making new ones and finding new avenues for networking. With a green pen she drew a small circle and then around the circle she drew another larger one. Once she had three circles, she then began writing names. Her closest friends from work she listed inside the smallest circle. They would be the foundation of her network. Then her acquaintances, like the other residents in the block that she knew well by sight but only really exchanged pleasantries with. These would actually be the most tricky, as it would be hard to overstep the polite distance everyone kept and also she didn't want to upset or fall out with them, as they could make things unpleasant, and her home was her sanctuary. Then lastly, in the outer circle she listed all the people who could be potential targets. People she hadn't met yet, like other mums in the same position as her who needed funds to pay for medical bills; the recently unemployed, who suddenly found themselves sinking into debt; addicts who all desperately needed money to feed their habit, whether it was drugs-related or because they had to have the latest 'props' accessories. These would be the easiest to approach, as she had nothing to lose. All she needed to do was find them and show them that the answer to their problems was right there, under their noses.

ANGUS

The table was filled with beautiful flowers. Not real, delicate blooms from the garden, but magical ones, created by Barney from rubbish and scraps people found and brought to him. Children, scavengers, looking for useful things to sell or recycle would also keep an eye out for short scraps of wire filament, bottle tops and tiny beads or broken coloured glass, that they knew Barney would view as treasures. He sat on his wheeled throne, busy at the table while his shiny prosthetic arms and fingers whirled industriously, soldering, clipping, cutting and moulding the waste products into the most delicate and intricate stamens and petals.

Angus loved nothing more than to while away the hours chatting and watching, as witnessing such creativity felt like devotional worship. His role in the community was still not certain, but there was no rush, no hurry, and everyone was keen for him to take his time getting to know them. He was given a series of rooms in a flat that had recently been left vacant. The previous occupant had been known and held in high regard by Aline, and after much discussion amongst the elders, it was felt to be a fitting residence for the new saviour. He spent little time in it, though, preferring to seek out company, as the thought of being alone freaked him out a bit.

He spent quite a bit of time observing and thinking how he could be useful, but none of his previous skills seemed appropriate in this new environment. He had thought at first that he might be a welcome military presence, but he soon realised that no one was interested in his muscle flexing and to be honest, neither was he. Eventually he stopped carrying his weapons around and only wore his natural prosthesis, although for a while it made him feel very vulnerable.

Aline made it clear that everyone was to return to their day-to-day routine and allow Angus to settle in. They knew he was a born leader and were simply waiting for him to discover what it was he would be leading them to, and then they would happily follow, but until his calling became clear, they were keen to show him around and show off their own skills.

They all had clear duties, and a deep loyalty and commitment to each other that meant these duties were never shirked. One of the duties was policing the area, which the teenage boys took on as they scouted the area on various contraptions that they spent hours tinkering with. They had simple but effective tactics. Any strangers were deterred by a sudden, complete absence of any sign of life. To the outside eye, the area looked deserted and almost eerily quiet as everyone disappeared to their inner rooms. Like rabbits and meerkats, they simply took to their burrows until the shadow of the predator passed by.

Angus spent some time assisting the boys who looked after the north of the precinct, who had been the first to spot him arriving.

"We knew just by your walk that you were someone. You know, not just anyone."

Aaron bragged. "I was up there." He pointed to the roof of an old bank that had once towered over the area. The building was no longer used, and the bank had relocated years ago. Shiny, rotating solar panels covered the structure from head to toe and it was impossible to see where anyone could stand to look out.

"Yeah, we said to each other, 'Let's not mess with this dude,' so we sent 'hold' messages out."

"Hold?" Angus queried.

"Yes, as in 'hold positions', it means don't do anything, keep out of sight until danger passes."

"But then you went into the room and sat on the bed," Roller sniggered. Roller had small wheels fitted on the bottom of his chunky plastic legs, with lots of complicated-looking springs and padding, which he claimed was for suspension. Quite a few of the boys were on wheels, but Roller was the first that they knew to have his installed.

"Dude, he didn't just sit on it, he lay on it!"

"Yeah, we couldn't believe it!"

"Phib went mental, you should have seen him!"

"Shut up, I didn't." Phib blushed. He rarely said anything, letting Aaron and Roller bicker things out.

"I'm very sorry to have done that, but I didn't realise it was taboo. Can you explain why the bed is sacred?"

Aaron looked down in reverential deference, "You just don't touch the bed. It's special."

"Yes, but why?"

"You just don't." Roller looked very serious and crossed himself hastily, as though even thinking about sitting on the bed was a sin.

Angus sighed. "Did the bed belong to someone important? Or is it being saved for someone?"

"Dude, you need to ask Aline. She'll explain it best."

"My dad might tell you; I'm worried I'll explain it wrong." Phib blushed again as the others stared at him.

"Then let's go and ask, come on." Roller set off.

"He works with the chickens," Phib confided proudly to Angus as they followed Roller to a tall brick building known as Ash Court, flanked by similar tower blocks, each indistinguishable from the other. Ash Court, Pine Rise, and the Fir Flats were built as a trio to form the base of the farming community, with sky walks to link between them. Despite their strong relationship and shared interests, each block was self-sufficient, with a smallholding on each roof with livestock such as goats, rabbits and chickens, as well as a basement for growing all types of fungi. Those who had chosen farming duties, like Phib's dad, seemed the most contented to Angus.

After some meaningful looks from the boys, Angus cleared his throat and asked, "I do hope you don't mind, but I would be interested to know what you can tell me about the bed?"

"Ah, well now, we have about five main beds divided into sections. As you can see, we are getting ready for planting in the spring, now that the snow has finally melted, but we're still heavily reliant on our greenhouse for all our food at the moment."

After momentary confusion, Angus allowed himself to be side-tracked; after all, there was no urgency to his question, he was just curious, and he assumed Aline would tell him as and when she felt he needed to know. Seeing the conversation sinking into rooftop agricultural vernacular, the boys disappeared to resume their vigil.

The garden was a heavenly cornucopia in miniature, in striking contrast to the wasteland below. Surprisingly large, it was divided into an area for fruit in cages and rows of vegetables, and also sections set aside for herb beds backed onto now-grubby space for sweet corn and artichokes at the back. A strict rotational system was used in planting, with brassicas following legumes, for example. Phib's dad tried to explain to Angus that it was to do with nitrogen levels and then showed him huge tubs of potatoes that would love the nitrogen-rich soil, but couldn't be planted alongside brassicas, as they needed different PH levels. Angus soon realised that he wasn't destined to be a farmer, as there were far too many different vegetables, all with different needs, and it was far too complicated. Give him a battle strategy any day.

Each of the tower blocks had a unique design. This one was pretty much fifty-fifty open air to glass ratio as they had livestock, but other blocks were either all open or all under glass, depending on what their farming speciality was.

Bees, goats and chickens all had their place in this roof garden and although Phib's dad was officially in charge of the chickens, he was obviously knowledgeable about the whole area.

"Look at her, beauty, isn't she? A rare sight these days. I'm hoping to breed her with the reds and rear a gang of Isa Browns."

Angus yet again had no idea what Phib's dad was talking about, but he admired the snow-white hen, who carefully picked her way through the bustle of dark, ruby red chickens at their feet.

"Loving things, these birds. My best friends, aren't you, ladies?"

They gave him a cackling reply, then squawked off to investigate a new heap of old weeds one of the gardeners chucked into their pen.

"There's a pecking order, isn't there, girls? You're the first to pick out the insects and small plants like clover, chickweed and dandelion. Then, when they've finished, the goats eat the rest."

Angus watched as the chickens ran in and out past the goats that snatched up the larger swathes of greens. It looked the other way round to him, as though the chickens were scavenging the leftovers.

Every now and then, a large, black rook would stop by, calling out to his mates to join him, then they'd hop about on the walls, daring each other to steal from the animals, until one of the younger children would rush at them, clanging tins to scare them off. Angus found his fingers itching to set off a few rounds at the birds but didn't have his weapons fitted, so joined the children in shouting and waving at them instead. The farmers were such a relaxed and friendly bunch he would soon get into the routine of spending hours with them, trying to make himself useful. He enjoyed the physical labour and sometimes he joined them helping funnel the waste from the top of the building to the bottom. In the basement, fungi broke the waste down rapidly so it could be reused as compost and the edible mushrooms were almost a by-product. The most excitement was when one of the rabbits broke free and Angus took the puppy up to help catch it. A rabbit in the cage was incredibly valuable, but one roaming free in the garden was a disaster!

It was a simple and rewarding life, held together by the ritual of the church and Aline's strong guidance.

It didn't seem as though the community needed Angus at all!

DETER

Someone had jammed one of the optic spirit dispensers, and now it dripped slowly but steadily, so you had to remember to put a clean glass underneath it every now and then. When it was full, you had to remove the bottle and open it, tip the overspill back in, then reattach it. This was just one of the many rather annoying glitches that afflicted the bar in The George. Another was that the spill drip tray under the lemonade tap had a leak, so you had to put an absorbent mat under it as no one seemed bothered to replace it. Deter had worked several shifts now and also found that each of her different workmates had a slightly different pricing system. Pip operated on a generous rounding down of figures, whereas Martha tended to do the opposite. None of the customers seemed to mind, and they waited patiently while Deter diligently added up everything correctly.

It was her first night to open up alone and she turned the taps to let the beer flow in from the kegs through long, rather grubby-looking tubes to the taps. The tubes seemed to disappear through walls, reappear along the floor and then go underground again. She couldn't work out which carried what, but she hadn't had to reattach a new barrel yet so she didn't bother her head about it. She siphoned off the first pint and began unstacking the dishwasher that was full of rows of now-clean lunchtime glasses.

After slicing the lemons and filling the icebox, she flipped through the song selection. There was nothing she knew, so she chose an artist based on name alone and idly flipped though the album.

"Oooh, good choice," a friendly voice said over her shoulder. She hadn't heard Martha come in and jumped a bit in surprise. "You were miles away! Everything looks ready, though, well done, we'll make a barmaid out of you yet. There's nothing quite like an English pub as the perfect location for setting the world to rights. Penny for them?"

"Um... I'm not quite sure what you mean?"

"It's an expression. I've no idea where it came from, but it means what are you thinking?"

"Actually, for the first time in a long time, I was thinking of absolutely nothing! Just wondering who this band is."

"Oh my God! You don't know who Jezebels Jewels are? Where've you been for the last five years?"

Deter winced internally, as Martha didn't talk; she shrieked or roared. The volume and energy always went up several notches when she walked in. "That's a pretty good question that I've been asking myself a lot recently." Deter grimaced; she really didn't need reminding of her messed-up existence.

"Sorry, I didn't mean it like that. It's just that they are huge! I know all the words to their first album, *Riding on a Jet Storm*. How can you not know 'Blinding'?" Martha took a huge breath, then burst into enthusiastic and very loud song, competing with the track that was already playing, "Let's put it on!" she cried, grabbing control of the sound system.

Soon she was dancing around the bar; Deter's spirits lifted as the music spiralled and soared around them. Martha didn't stop dancing even when the first customer arrived, making them wait until the end of the track before collapsing in an exhausted, hot, happy heap on one of the bar stools.

"I need a drink!" Martha exclaimed as she fanned herself with a beermat. "Anyone know a good pub round here?"

"The George used to be good, until the barmaids started fancying themselves as pop stars," the customer replied dryly as he seated himself down.

"Shut up, Ryan! You wouldn't have me any other way. Your usual?"

Ryan nodded as Martha expertly poured a pint. "Even though you rob me blind! You should rename this establishment 'The Highwayman.'"

Martha tutted as Deter looked slightly anxiously between the two. Sometimes it was hard to tell if English people were joking.

"This is Ryan. Don't let him give you any trouble. He's all mouth and no trousers." Martha wiped away a slight dribble of beer, then stood, resting her ample cleavage on the top of the bar. "Any luck selling your house yet?"

"No, sadly no one wants a run-down flat in Dray Walk. Too many properties all the same and everyone is spoilt for choice." Ryan took a long draught of his beer and smacked his lips greedily.

"I'd love it, but it's too big for me. I can't afford anything unless I move in with someone and I'm not ready for the commitment. Besides, I love having loads of people around me. Being on me own gives me the collywobbles. Communal living makes sense on all levels: it's cheap and a continual party!" Martha jiggled and kicked up her heels, bursting into song again.

"What do you think, Deter? You have to admit London is pretty cool. New York might be the Big Apple, but we're the bee's knees, the big cheese, the golden goose—"

"The dog's bollocks?"

"Now, now, Ryan, no need for that sort of language! Deter is our guest. We don't want her to think we're uncultured."

Martha mock-frowned and whipped Ryan gently with her dishrag. Deter sighed; this was obviously Martha's way with the clientele. She would never be able to be so upbeat and familiar.

As the evening progressed, the pub filled up, and Deter was so busy her head was filled with nothing but orders at the bar and a dizzying cycle of stacking and emptying of the dishwasher. By the end of the evening she was exhausted but feeling positive as she was learning so much. The small details of the job, which were really easy in theory, required her to take initiative and use her common sense, which she hadn't really had to do before. It made her realise how much Amery had sheltered her. So many types of people, all expecting her to know their preferences and interests and engage in fast-paced small talk with limitless enthusiasm; it was exhausting, but rewarding. She felt she was contributing and starting to pay her way.

Deter had decided not to let Pip have her monitor. She knew that the Faction would find it an incredibly valuable asset, but it was hers. She felt strongly that Jameson had wanted her to keep it and it sat comfortably in her pocket, a secret she could reach for when she felt homesick and needed comfort. She didn't talk to Lincoln about it and she hoped he wouldn't mention it, as he would probably make her feel guilty for holding on to it. The Faction's cause meant far more to him than it did to her. Deter felt more loyalty to Lincoln himself and the Faction back home. Although she was starting to get used to everyone here in England, she wished more than anything she could turn back time and go back to her old life.

While Lincoln worked in the laboratory with Pip's uncle at St Peters, Deter had quite a few spare hours in between shifts. She spent these either in the gym recharging the house battery packs or her own personal one, or exploring the area. One of her favourite buildings shone out golden, a blonde among the redheads, drawing you in through its huge stone archway. A gallery for many centuries, international artists such as Picasso, Rothko and Frieda Kahlo had exhibited there. It was now divided into quiet space to research and enjoy the old reference material, or a busy, noisy hub of community creativity. Faction members spent a great deal of time here, chatting to members of the local community. It was a way to gently canvas and network and explore and share ideas. Touring exhibitions, as well as emerging artists' work was exhibited still, and each room was carefully curated to lead you through a varied sensory experience.

She spent increasingly more time with Martha and her friends, and she found that Martha's confidence was rubbing off on her. Martha had joined the Faction when she was very young, as her parents were both active members. When her father left her mother and began a long, drawn-out bitter divorce, Martha spent more time with her Faction extended family than either her mother or father. Dad was still active but with a new partner who ran a pod in Camden, and Mum had moved away out of London to a commune in the hilly Cotswolds.

The thing Deter liked best about her was that she was nothing like Jenny and Padma. She missed her friends greatly but was so glad that Martha liked doing completely different things. Jenny and Padma would have taken a trip straight up to Bond Street and shopped the hell out of it. In the Whitechapel Gallery they would have spent more time in the café and gift shop than looking at exhibits, and they certainly wouldn't have taken part in making a wire and plaster sculpture. London with them would be amazing but ramped up with unlimited dollars.

Now she felt so proud as she plugged in her battery pack to heat the water for her shower. She had to be quick washing as she promised to help Martha start preparing for the annual Faction pantomime. It was another of their creative projects that had political undertones, an ancient way of spreading propaganda behind a benign disguise. The antagonists always had thinly veiled associations with the Establishment, either names, or characteristics that could be easily recognised and made into caricatures. Almost everyone she had talked to couldn't wait to watch it, but very few actually wanted to be in it. Even Pip, who as a trained actor should have been the first to audition, was often too busy. Plus, more fun was in watching and heckling! So, it seemed as though pretty much the same cast volunteered year on year.

"So, this is last year's programme so you can see who was in it. Brian wants to be the Dame again, but I'm not sure I can take the stress of him not knowing his lines."

"If he doesn't do it, who would be suitable?" Deter peered at the grainy photo of an ageing man with a huge red beard, full make-up and a ruffled floral cap, perched precariously on russet ringlets. She had heard of pantomimes but never seen one. She knew the Dame was usually always a man dressed as a woman and the Principle Boy was a girl. It was the one art form that would have even the most politically correct and prejudiced laughing together, despite the cross-dressing and risqué nature of the scripts.

"Well, that's the problem, no one really, apart from me! But as wonderful as I am, I can't play every role. I'm already playing the part of Buttons as well as producing and directing." Martha tried to look outraged and modest simultaneously, but just went slightly pink and her breasts seemed to inflate to double the size.

"Maybe I could help by spending extra time with Brian to help him with his lines? He does look splendid in a dress!" Deter giggled as she pointed to an excellent photo of Brian centre-stage, attempting what looked like the can-can.

"That would be a huge help, and yes, he was fabulous on the night. The other issue is that our potential Cinderella can't dance."

"Does she need to? Surely others could sort of dance around her?"

"That's true, if we are clever with choreography, she could just be moved about by everyone else."

"When do we start rehearsals?" Deter could feel herself getting caught up in it and was looking forward to getting to know some of the others better.

"Well, we try and do it in between shifts. So late afternoons and some evenings when it's quiet, we learn lines and songs in the bar. The punters love it, and they often come and see it, as they've been watching it take shape."

"That's good, maybe Lincoln would like to join in."

"I really don't think he's performance material," Martha said very seriously. Seeing Deter's face, she added conciliatorily, "We could put him in charge of props, though, if you think he'd like to be involved."

Deter had been about to volunteer for one of the chorus girls, but now fretted that Martha would reject her. "I will very happily be a sounding board, and any little jobs you need doing, just ask. I'll also go through lines, of course."

"Marvellous! It's just the best time of the year! We have six weeks then we open on the first of April!"

Deter was sitting in a café just next to the Whitechapel Gallery going over Brian's lines with him when she heard a faint click and buzz that sounded like a camera focussing. She looked up and saw a man taking shots of the street with his camera, but as he pushed down on the shutter, the noise was somehow different. She angled her head towards where she thought the sound had come from, but there was nothing. Unsettled, she had lost her place in the script, and Brian was foundering and wildly gesturing for her to prompt him.

"Really, Deter, darling, how am I supposed to learn my lines if you don't concentrate?" Brian fussed, slightly irrationally. "Now I'll have to start again."

A big man with a magnificent beard, he also had interesting scarring from an accident years ago when a friend threw a large rock at him and it caught his cheek. It left an unsightly indent, but you only noticed it once you were close as the beard rather stole the show. He worked for a graphics company and produced most of the Faction's visual propaganda.

As he launched forth, still on Act 1, Scene 1, Deter heard the noise again. It was definitely coming from her left, slightly behind her. She swivelled to examine the wall and Brian, losing his thread completely, threw up his hands and went to order another coffee.

The wall was ordinary brick with nothing especially interesting about it. Deter methodically scanned up and down it, looking for a glassy lens as she was sure she was being watched, but there was nothing there. Sighing, she shrugged it off and tried to absorb herself in the play. When Brian returned, brandishing cinnamon mochas, she made an extra effort to give him one hundred per cent of her attention.

At that night's rehearsal, she was proud and gratified that

Brian was one of the most confident with his lines, and she basked in Martha's effusive praise. As Martha paced in front of the stage, watching every movement her cast made with a critical eye, Deter and Lincoln started sifting through old props and costumes.

The props and costumes were housed in one of the storerooms in an attic accessed from the end of one of the creaky corridors. They had to stand on a chair to lift the square ceiling panel off before pulling down an old fold-out ladder. Up there were boxes of rather smelly, jumbled-up clothes and old programmes; a couple of dusty awards, dating back years; and also, rather frighteningly, a realistic skeleton wearing bits of armour.

"Oh, yes, we had him propped up in the corner of Ali Baba's cave last year. He's so cool, isn't he? We call him Nigel."

Martha hadn't stayed long up there with them and hadn't ever returned, asking for every potential item to be brought down instead.

Lincoln had initially been reluctant to join in the pantomime preparations, as he was exhausted when he got back from the hospital, but he was starting to find it an excellent way to switch off after a day examining group A *Streptococcus bacteria*. His head was spinning with the tricky sequence patterns of multiple protein strains and was now doubting his theory that Deter's DNA held the key. He had truly believed that whatever it was in Deter's system that combated the disease could be isolated and used to help create the vaccine. Now he wasn't so sure. He wasn't sure it was possible to create a vaccine at all.

"Look at this! These are so cute!" Deter had pulled out a box of gnome hats with white beards already attached.

"I'm not sure that Doc, Grumpy and Sleepy are invited to Cinderella's ball!" Lincoln replied.

"But they could be really funny for the one of the dances! We need these, though." She pulled out a huge pair of wings and several wands and tiaras. "Ideal for our Fairy Godmother."

They set aside a series of waistcoats and an elaborate frock coat, as well as flower garlands for the village chorus, and then lugged it down the hatch. After receiving Martha's approval, even for the gnomes' hats, they then spent the rest of the evening repairing the waistcoats and making sure all the flower garlands looked fresh and new.

As they wiped the dust off each petal with a damp cloth, Deter felt the beginnings of contentment. She looked up at Lincoln and smiled. "Who knew, just a few months ago, that we'd be halfway across the world! I still can't believe that everyone I knew then has disappeared from my life. I'm in a new place, with new people, thrown into a world full of all sorts of adventures. I've sort of got over the shock, I think, and am getting used to being here." She looked over at Martha and deliberately raised her voice to add teasingly, "Apart from Martha's shocking taste in music… I'll never get over that!"

"I heard that!" Martha interjected, looking up from her directorial notes to shoot a jokingly stern glance at Deter.

"I know, and I hope you're OK with no fixed plan, as I'm not sure what's happening with the vaccine. We haven't made the progress we hoped for." Lincoln lowered his voice and looked embarrassed. "I've turned your life upside down and it might have been for nothing."

"Don't be silly, nothing is ever for nothing and you haven't been working on it for long. You mustn't give up!"

"No, I haven't, it's just, it's much less straightforward than I thought. The FED virus is just unbelievably complex."

"Well, at the moment we have more pressing issues." Deter threw a fraying garment at him. "See? Prince Charming won't be so charming if his waistcoat is unravelling. Get to work and see if you can doctor that!"

So Lincoln allowed Deter to pull him into a less frantic and almost domestic pace. They spent their evenings socialising with the others in the large communal space or working shifts in The George. There was a continual gentle buzz of political activity that trotted on in a sedate way. A few posters here and there, pro-Faction-based conversations at local community events, grassroots stuff, but nothing thrusting and urgent like the work in New York. Deter went on regular seed-bombing days to 'spread the love', as Annabel put it, and helped out at local soup kitchens where gangs with no prosthetics suddenly emerged fast and furious on various makeshift vehicles. There was a warmth and happiness that spread to everyone living in the Faction community, mainly due to Pip's benign leadership. Everyone felt they had their place and was valued, and it meant that as a unit they were incredibly loyal and strong.

The only worm in the apple was a growing paranoia that something or someone was watching her. Every now and then, Deter's hairs on the back of her neck would stand up, and a prickly feeling would spread over her back. She was convinced that she heard the click of cameras and that tell-tale whir as a camera refocussed. It could happen in quite unlikely places, like on routine shopping trips. She could be coming back from the market and crossing over the road past the Indian confectionary shop when a glint of reflected light flashed out the corner of her eye. Turning to see it, it would then be impossible to locate, but the sense of being observed froze her inside.

ANGUS

A new feeling of unrest was creeping into the Brownsville community and Angus almost didn't notice it. He was so relaxed into his new way of life that his senses could easily have chosen to ignore the small, subtle signs that things were changing.

As winter turned into spring, wildflowers sprung up, pushing their way through the slightest weakness in the concrete, fighting their way out of the darkness into the sun. High above, the cultivated gardens began to put out green shoots and the children ran shrieking at the increasing number of birds to warn them that scavengers were not welcome.

Barney had begun to take his creations outside and throughout the summer, the residents were uplifted as new intricate designs greeted them on their day-to-day travels.

He planted his recycled flowers in colourful drifts, brightening up the most neglected areas and Barney took great satisfaction when real plants became entwined in his metal ones as the concept somehow amused him. "Life imitating art and vice versa," he would say happily.

But as the days began to heat up, the intensity of the sun suddenly went from pleasant to too much and made the boys on lookout irritable. Foolish would be the wanderer to enter the barren wasteland east of the city. A hot, bothered Roller was not as tolerant as a cool, laid-back one!

Things above remained the same, as the children and the farmers continued their cycle of seasons with the exhausting but rewarding job of keeping everyone from starvation, but amongst the young men and young women on the ground, there was a new restlessness.

Aaron had started talking about pushing boundaries into Crown Heights and was spending a lot of time hanging around the woodland off Rochester Avenue and acting as though his very presence was an expression of ownership. He talked about Eastern Parkway as though it was the gateway to Manhattan Bridge, which in itself was taking on a new revered symbolism. No one had really bothered to explore much beyond the community until now, at least not for a long time. Their self-sufficiency in terms of both physical and spiritual nourishment had been untested and accepted for many years. Angus's arrival signified change, but he himself was only just getting used to things as they were.

Aline and the other elders knew from experience that time solves everything and were content to let the boys test their boundaries. Any concerns they had, they kept to themselves. This was an age-old problem echoed for centuries in the behaviour of wild animals: a marking of territory, a display of power. It was one of those things that would work itself out.

But there was something else going on that was much more worrying.

For decades the disabilities caused by FED had led to the innovative technology to replace lost limbs growing into an enormous industry. Those who could afford it bought high-tech, all-singing, all-dancing toys to enhance their abilities and overcompensate for their loss. But now, filtering down into mainstream was high-end fashion for natural prosthetics. This desire to look Complete was something only the richest could afford, but it was starting to filter down into the rest of the community. Realistic limbs appeared on high-profile celebrities, but the real obsession was with transplants and where there's demand, supply follows.

It was Barney who first noticed that some of the poorest people were disappearing for a period of time, only to emerge weeks later with even more disabilities. It wasn't until old Margaret came back without her signature limp but with a newly missing arm that he mentioned what he'd found out to Angus. "I knew she hadn't had an accident, as someone would have said, so I asked her what happened? Where did she lose her arm? I knew something didn't seem right."

He paused as he lifted a huge cluster of bell-like blooms attached to a metal stake and moved them pedantically three inches to the right. He was really into spring wildflowers that hung from stems in bell shapes: harebells, bluebells, snowdrops, lily of the valley, and bleeding heart. He had created large, bright clusters suspended from curved stems that looked stunning alone and incredibly dramatic en masse. He was arranging a swathe of blue stems by the front of the church's entrance and working on staggering heights and distances.

"Margaret told me she was finally out of debt and that the stress of that had been such a burden. She's also not the only one," he continued. "She told me that some of the other poorer members of the community are also selling their remaining limbs. It's awful and full of unnecessary risks, but they feel it's worth it."

"Did you just say selling them?" Angus interrupted. He was shocked.

"Yes, the money is amazing, so seductive. When you think of the medical bills that some of us have, it seems a worthwhile solution." Barney sat up and wiped his brow. He reversed and faced Angus, who looked unbelievably worried. "We can't stop progress I suppose," he said.

"But is this progress?" Angus frowned. "I'm not saying things can't change. Everyone needs to improve their lives if they can, but when is progress a good thing and when does it become a reflection of unhealthy aspirations? I can't help but feel people are being taken advantage of."

"I dunno, it's their choice, and money is pretty rare here, as you know. We barter and get by, but who wouldn't want more if they could?"

There was something in Barney's tone that made Angus examine him closer. "But you're happy, aren't you, Barney?"

Barney straightened up from tending his flowerbed to gaze at some point in the distance. "I just want my art to be recognised a bit further afield than Brownsville. How amazing it would be to have an exhibition in the Lisson, for instance."

The Lisson! Wow! Of course, Barney, like all artists, wanted recognition. Not wealth or commercial success, but accolades from respected connoisseurs from the world of modern art. No one had ever asked Barney what he wanted from life until now, and it was only recently that he had acknowledged certain desires. Like Aaron, he wanted to conquer new ground. He was known and respected as the residential artist here with very little competition, but beyond the boundaries of this neighbourhood, he had no idea how his work stood up against his contemporaries.

"But this could happen, right? Why don't you submit some work?" Angus said.

"Look at me. I'm not the sort of person who is accepted over there. I haven't had formal training; I don't know the right language."

"It's art! Surely it speaks for itself?"

"Maybe, I just wouldn't know how to even begin," said Barney.

Angus sat back in thought. Nothing was stopping Barney, was it? Except himself? He had these unidentified barriers that made it easier for him to be non-proactive. But the desire was there. A desire for more; a need that was unfulfilled.

Barney wanted to be appreciated and have his talents recognised by significant movers and shakers in the art world. This was a very common desire and there was no reason why it couldn't be achieved.

The most sinister change in the community was this swift rise out of poverty through the sale of body parts. It was upsetting the long-established hierarchical harmony. Suddenly, some people had a great deal more money than others. Communal rations were being supplemented by delicious ingredients bought from elsewhere, and the other residents had to smell and hear of these mouth-watering delights. New fashions from the city were being worn and there was a feeling of being 'old-fashioned' and 'out of date' that the community had never suffered from before. Those who could now afford it started travelling further afield, not just for clothes and food but leisure activities as well, and the whole of Brownsville was infected by a greed they hadn't experienced before. More troubling were the after effects of the donations. Despite top-quality care, several residents had died, as they were simply too old or unwell to have donated. Amputation was a major and serious operation and despite the outward health of these patients, the clinic should have refused to operate. Heart complications, deep vein thrombosis and pneumonia were all life-threatening side effects.

Angus felt he needed to talk to Aline about it, as he felt the church should play a pivotal role in guiding its flock through this potential crisis. It was truly appalling that people were being taken advantage of, and he resolved to get to the root of the problem. Targeting people because of their poverty was a pretty low thing to do in his book. It was illegal to pay for donations and the loophole regarding *expenses* ought to be closed. But he was only one man, and a failed activist at that, how was he going to change anything?

Needing more time to reflect and ponder the issues, he took the lift up to Ash Court, where Phib's dad was wheeling large quantities of compost to the indoor beds. It was tiring and repetitive work, but Angus took over and then joined in, pushing tiny seeds into trays and labelling everything carefully. The rows of salad leaves would start coming up soon and another set would need to be planted in two weeks' time. Once they were transplanted outdoors, they would have chives and garlic in between them to keep aphids at bay. He wished that the world was as orderly and productive as the rooftop gardens. He had learnt so much in the recent months up here with the farmers. Disease was kept in check and ruthless culling sometimes needed to stop the spread. Blight, for instance, affected potatoes and could wipe out a whole crop within days. Instant panic had swept through the farmers when early blight was detected. Tell-tale brown spots on the leaves meant the whole crop was lost. Angus had helped rip out the infected plants and destroy them. Using disease-free seed potatoes or using blight-resistant varieties was the only solution. But they thought they'd taken those precautions. How had it happened? But then, wasn't that what the Establishment had been trying to do with the human race? Maybe it wasn't such an unethical solution after all. Their plans for breeding Deter with another Immune could have worked. Maybe it was the natural and only way forward for survival of the fittest. Protective fungicide could also be used, which was similar to what the Faction had wanted: a vaccine to prevent disease setting in. But unlike blight, at least there was a cure for FED, even though it came with terrible side effects.

Maybe the answers are all up here, thought Angus, looking around at the freshly turned earth waiting for new seedlings to be planted. This new trend of having limb transplants was, he supposed similar, to grafting roses. A new plant springing from old stock and hybrids emerging, bringing the best from different types of species. But unlike roses, limb transplants were only cosmetic. It wouldn't change the breeding stock and wouldn't enhance future generations.

Sighing, he travelled back down to earth, hoping to find Aline to talk things through with. He deeply regretted his treatment of Deter and assumed she was probably buried beneath the rubble alongside his men at the Faction's headquarters. Without Immunes like her, the human race was never going to be able to breed the disease out. He had felt almost afraid of her because her purity was almost freaky. He remembered looking down at the burning heap of brown, rotting potatoes, and he now suspected that it was the rest of mankind who were to be feared. He had prodded a tuber that had fallen from the pile and a revolting liquid had oozed out. The stench had been quite appalling. In a fearsome moment of revelation, Angus saw the future of the human race.

Down amongst the brick and concrete pathways, small, candle-like buds were pushing up between the cracks, and as spring progressed, they opened into purple flowers with the brightest yellow stamens. Disproportionately large for the flower, the bright yellow anthers loaded with pollen called out cheerfully to bees emerging from their winter cluster.

Stumbling past on his way to find Aline, Angus didn't even see the crocuses, and at least five small blooms were left crushed under his size nine boots.

DETER

Deter had put the monitor away, tucked inside an old but beautiful box she had found in the market. She had been keeping it on her at all times since her arrival in England but was starting to relax and trust her new friends. She didn't think they would ever take it without asking, so she knew it would be quite safe there. The box had ornate patterns carved into it and delicate filigree panels embedded on the lid. It was the sort of thing you want to touch, and she often stood reflecting on her day while tracing the decorative lines. She had wanted to show Lincoln and for him to enjoy the tactile experience, but then hesitated, unsure of how effective his prosthetics were.

He had laughed at her anxiety and immediately shown her the mechanics of his arms. "See here, in the back of my head, is a small scar. That's where a chip is inserted that links my brain up with my arms. I can feel pretty much everything I could before I lost my limbs, as my brain transfers all my memories into my prosthetics. So, for example, I touch this, and my brain knows it's going to be bumpy, so I can feel it is bumpy."

"That's amazing, but do you still miss your old body?"

"What wouldn't I give for my old body! No dodgy heart, for a start."

"Yeah, but it's pretty cool to be able to see it beating." Deter placed her hand on his chest and smiled as they both felt it begin to race at her touch. She lifted his T-shirt to witness it beating and then kissed him gently to watch the pace of his heart rocket.

"That's totally not fair," he smiled, "but my heart is on borrowed time, so don't wear it out."

"What's that supposed to mean?"

"Nothing serious, but most of my organs are either diseased or already replaced. It's just one of those things."

"Well, it sounds very serious. How easy is it to get replacements?"

"I haven't looked into it. I'm not sure how it works here, but in New York, you're on a list. First come, first served."

"Where do the organs come from?"

"Where do you think?"

"But that's awful! So someone has to die before you can inherit their organs. Why can't they make them in a laboratory or something?"

"That's not ethical, Deter. That would be cloning, and cloning cannot be justified."

"Oh really? Yet here I am!"

"That's different, Deter, you're different."

"But I'm a clone and so, therefore, unethical and unjustified. Your words, Lincoln, your words!"

Their first row and Lincoln didn't know what to do. He wanted to undo the last part of the conversation and go back to the kiss but didn't know how. He wanted to put his arms around her, but from the stiffness in her back and her refusal to look at him, he thought it best to turn and leave the room instead.

Alone, Deter felt the emptiness acutely. How could things have gone from flirty to firey so quickly? She had immediately regretted flaring up at Lincoln, but he had reminded her that she was unusual just as she was beginning to fit in. The preciousness of life and the worry for their health was something everyone had to deal with every day, and she felt almost guilty for not having the same concerns. Guilty and also at the same time left out, not in the club. It was a funny mix of feelings and left her feeling even lonelier.

"Oh, Jameson, I wish I was eating breakfast with you, chatting while we wait for Amery to arrive. Everything was so simple then."

She wept quietly as she thought back to the life she had lost. She wondered what Jenny and Padma were doing. Did they miss her too? She would ask Lincoln to search for news of them again. Then she remembered she had fallen out with Lincoln and cried new fresh tears.

Needing comfort, she took the monitor back out of the box, wanting the reassurance of seeing her beloved city again. Opening it up, she admired the miniature details and clasped it tightly in her hands as though she could impress the outline of the city forever on her skin. On impulse, she pressed the button on the side and watched as the city opened up, filling the room with its familiar architectural lines. She stood in the middle of Central Park and shut her eyes, rotating slowly as in her mind's eye she recalled every vista that she stored in her memory.

Smiling and beginning to relax, she opened her eyes, but to her horror she was no longer standing in Central Park. Instead, the newly familiar buildings of Whitechapel and Bethnall

Green sprung up. She checked the monitor and the tiny replica of New York was still there, but the city surrounding her most definitely was not. Horrified, she quickly shut it down and debated what to do next.

It had been an excellent rehearsal, and Martha had organised for the cast to go out for a few drinks somewhere a 'bit swanky', as she put it. They were buoyed up by the excellent last few hours where the whole play was finally put together. All the little scenes and songs and dances that each group had been working on separately had been strung together and, amazingly, ran smoothly and on time. The first few performances had sold well, but the last few had quite a few empty seats, so tonight's celebration would also include canvassing. Brian armed everyone with a bunch of leaflets each and they were giving out flyers as they went, chatting and singing excerpts to entice people to buy tickets. It was vital that the play do well, as it was an important tool for their political propaganda.

Deter didn't enjoy leaving the safety of the Faction, as the feeling of being watched had increased. She looked nervously around her and couldn't relax and enjoy herself the way the others were. Constantly on the alert for signs of cameras observing her, she stuck close to Lincoln. Their argument now forgotten, he was the only person she had confided her fears to, as she knew he wouldn't dismiss them as unfounded paranoia.

He was also the only person she had shown the monitor's changed status to. They had checked the new map together, and after plugging the device in to a computer, they discovered that it lit up, showing cameras pretty much on every street corner. It looked as though Deter had inadvertently triggered all the cameras by walking past nearly every day with the monitor in her pocket. As they turned into Bethnal Green

Road from Brick Lane, Deter knew a camera was coming up and tried to locate it. She deliberately looked up to where it should be and waved defiantly.

"What are you doing?" Lincoln hissed, trying not to let the others hear.

"Well, they must know that we know they are there," Deter reasoned.

"Yes, but that doesn't mean that waving is a good idea."

"I'm sick of the whole thing. I need to know who they are and what they want," Deter replied.

"And what if you don't like the answer?"

"Anything is better than not knowing."

She continued stopping at every camera location and waving when out of sight of the others. As she was waving at a wall outside The Goblin while the others were already inside ordering cocktails, a woman with very short, dark hair and a limp came towards her. It looked as though the woman was about to approach her, but Brian burst through the door, brandishing a pink drink with several huge straws that fell out onto the pavement.

"Whoops! There goes the pina from your colada! Enjoy, darling, you've been such a marvel, I don't think we've ever been so prepared for opening night!"

The woman took a jump to the side to avoid the falling straws and after a furtive sideways glance at Deter, she hurried away.

"Oh! Thanks… um…" Deter turned to watch the woman hurrying away and kept her in her sight, as she was sure the woman would turn and look back at her, and if she did, then she was right and the woman had been intending to approach her. Sipping her drink from the last remaining straw, she smiled and nodded, only half-listening to Brian and then, just before she reached the corner of the street, the woman turned to look back at her. It was a sad and unsettling glance, and Deter felt profoundly disturbed by it. The whole night out had started with a really uncomfortable experience and she wished she had stayed in her room tucked up with some last-minute sewing repairs to the costumes. She took another sip of her rather delicious fruity drink and then, as the crushed ice in the bottom blocked up her straw, she realised she'd finished it already.

"Steady on, girl, the night is young, we don't want you to end up legless, especially as so many of us already are!" Brian guffawed rather tastelessly at her. "Another drink for our young friend," he shouted, handing her glass back to the crowd behind.

Oh, why not? she thought. Might as well enjoy the evening, and the alcohol was soothing the jittery feeling of being stalked. As another drink was pressed into her hand, she raised it up to meet Brian's.

"To politics, pantomime and pina coladas!" he cried merrily.

"The three 'p's… pitch, pace and projection!" Martha interrupted, raising the volume another decibel before she swept back into the throng, taking the party atmosphere with her.

"Typical director, always has to have the last word." Brian winked.

ANGUS

Voice sore from his last speech, Angus collapsed into bed, exhausted. He hoped that his people understood.

The dog was taking up most of his bed, so he curled himself around it and put up with a passionate kiss as the pup woke up enough to greet him, then fell back snoring.

He had thought long and hard about how to bring about change. It didn't matter who the people were behind the limb collection, the problem was with the demand. It was the people who wanted limb transplants that needed to be stopped. Whatever law is put in place, there will always be loopholes. Quick research had shown that at least twenty people from their church alone had already sacrificed a limb in the past two months. Who blamed them? The temptation was too strong and no man given the chance to make an easy buck was going to pass it up.

The wealthy elite who paid for the limbs were the ones who needed to be confronted. Aaron was going to be happy;

it was time to march from Brownsville across the Manhattan Bridge into the heart of New York.

Earlier, he had addressed the congregation for the first time. The huge meeting room had been filled to maximum capacity as word got around that Angus was making his inaugural speech. As trusting faces filled with anticipation lifted towards him, he felt a deep responsibility as well as a quivering of unexpected nerves.

"Our friends have died. Cate, our much-loved nursery nurse, died three weeks ago. Ferdinand only last week, his tables and chairs are now in most of our homes. Why? Because the divide between the prosperous elite and the underprivileged in America is wider than it has ever been," he began, straight to the point. "It was estimated that when the FED crisis first hit, those who inherited family wealth almost quadrupled their income, whereas those with nothing were left with nothing," he continued reassuringly as several people in the front two rows exchanged worried glances. "It's not just about money, it's about power and the assumption that we are willing to sell whatever money can buy."

This was inflammatory and he could tell that his audience, although surprised by the tone of his words, was in agreement, and energy was building in the room.

"Nothing is more valuable than what God gave you." Now he had them. "He gave you your mind and free will and although He took parts of our bodies, those were His to take. What He has left us, we should value and treasure."

"Amen." *Yes!* Now they were up on their feet.

He raised his voice slightly and spoke with utter conviction. "It's time to tear down the global elite who insist on living in an unrealistic bubble. I've been there. I've seen how they aspire to live as though FED doesn't exist. No one dares to show their disabilities there as it might upset the ladies while they are lunching. Children there have nothing to fear, only the best medical care and most realistic prosthetics. And now they want *our* bodies."

He had to shout to be heard over the cheers of assent. Raising his hands to quieten them, he lowered his voice in humility. "I have spent my life fighting. I came to you a battle-weary soldier who lost the war against the Establishment. But this time we fight with words and with our feet..." he smiled at Roller, "...or wheels!"

He pointed to the boys lounging in the corner; Aaron and a couple of other kids were balanced on a bookshelf, as the pews were full. "Aaron and Roller sit at the very borders of our neighbourhood." The boys sniggered, pleased to be singled out. "Their presence makes a statement. We are here. We are in charge, and we are taking over. The power of their physical presence is enough to send a message to the boys in Crown Heights. Who knows how the message will be answered!"

Someone punched Aaron teasingly on the back and he fell off his perch, which set everyone giggling again. They quickly refocussed as Angus's purpose unfolded.

"Meanwhile, we want to send a message to those ruling classes who think it's OK to exploit our vulnerable friends and family. We mustn't let them feel they can get away with it. How many of you knew that Barney dreams of exhibiting his work at the Lisson?" Barney looked down, not so keen to be singled out, so Angus moved swiftly on. "How many of you have actually been there? And why not? Who says that it's an impossible dream? Well, at the moment, Barney himself is saying so, because of how he believes he is seen, because he isn't already familiar with that world. Well, we are going to march from the comfort of our own homes to the heart of their community and make them as uncomfortable as possible.

Send word to your loved ones and let them know that we have had enough of being ignored and forgotten."

He had left the church with everyone buzzing with excitement. Everyone wanted a date to focus on, but he refused to be pinned down. Keen to stay and chat, there was soon food and music as the service turned into one of their famous impromptu parties. Now that the gates of unrest had been opened, he was overwhelmed by how many complaints people had about the wealthiest members of New York society. From the reasonable (especially the healthcare and education aspects) to the unreasonable (Margaret was convinced that her cat's death was a conspiracy), his mind was left in overdrive. Everyone was united in their anger over Cate and Ferdinand's deaths, and scared for their futures. Scenarios were discussed, especially using Barney as an example, imagining him as a boy from a privileged background and the path his life could have taken. Little snippets of conversation replayed through his racing thoughts.

While Angus walked the pup, tracing the now-familiar terrain in an effort to unwind, Aaron and Roller were still up, piecing the evening's events together.

"You need to be financially secure to be able to create," Roller mused, "or at least be free from having to channel your efforts into a job you don't want. That's what Miriam said. That's why she's cleans for us, it's not too demanding mentally so she still has energy to write songs for us."

"She said that to me too." Aaron nodded.

"I'd be a writer too if I didn't have to be on lookout," Roller continued cautiously. Aaron raised an eyebrow. "Knew you'd make a face like that." Roller sighed.

"Like what?" Aaron kicked him. "Do it! You could do both. Lots of the time nothing's happening."

"Yeah, but what if I was thinking about what I was writing and didn't notice someone coming? I often think about the stories I could write but haven't started yet. They are in here, but there's no quiet time to reflect and actually get them on paper."

"Phib could double up with you. Or we could recruit."

"Maybe." Roller looked pleased. At least Aaron hadn't laughed. "Barney is valued here, though, he lives with our support and is appreciated. Dunno what he's complaining about."

"That's not fair, he isn't complaining. It's not about us and how much we like his flowers. We aren't important in the art world. Barney wants professional validation."

"I sort of get it."

"You should, you're the one that wants to write. Imagine your stories read the world over."

"Wow!"

"Exactly, now imagine just us, me reading them."

"Point taken, anyway, we don't really need to get it, we just need to rebalance the way things are so we all have equal chances."

They sat thinking for a minute. Roller gently rocking to and fro on his wheels, and Aaron with his arms tight against his chest.

"I feel quite angry, don't you?" Aaron blurted out, kicking Roller's wheels.

"Oi, I know, don't take it out on me. We've been content to be sidelined, but we won't put up with being exploited."

"Yeah! Too right!"

"Time to invade Manhattan!"

"Can't wait!"

DETER

"I just want to try," Deter said firmly, as Lincoln shook his head worriedly.

"You're asking for trouble. The problem is, what if we don't like who is behind it?"

"That's sort of irrelevant. Whether we like them or not, they've gone to a lot of trouble to track us down. All those cameras! The resetting of the monitor, it's all been to watch me. At the moment, all the balls are in their court."

They sat thinking and looking at each other, hoping to find the answers from each other and drawing strength from their shared dilemma. Deter's eyes looked so haunted and sad that Lincoln could feel her isolation and paranoia just by gazing into them.

"I know, I should just ignore it. I should accept I'm being watched and just shrug it off, but it's too hard."

Lincoln continued looking at her as she tried to battle her fear and anxiety. He reached out and took her hand, gently but with resolution. "Are you certain you want to know who they are?" Lincoln paused, waiting for affirmation from Deter. She nodded. "Then we link it up to a computer, and wait and see if they try and talk to us."

Deter looked as if she was about to interrupt, but Lincoln held up his hand, asking her to wait. "You're not going to get anywhere just waving at the cameras. We need a computer to link the monitor up to, but we can't use any of the Faction's and we daren't return here once we've done it. If we establish contact, we can't risk endangering anyone else. Understood?"

Deter nodded.

"Also," Lincoln continued, "We do not initiate conversation. I can't stress that enough."

"What if no one answers first time? Can we come back here then?"

"No, I think we must decide whether we are staying here to help create the vaccine or moving on."

"We can't abandon the vaccine, though! Why are you so intent on severing our ties to everyone here? They are all we have."

"Look what happened last time. The whole New York unit went down. Progress is slow, but I think we are close, though. Plus, they have plenty of your blood samples, and the team is incredible, they won't miss me."

"The other option is that we wave at that camera by The Goblin and hope that the woman comes back."

"She might have nothing to do with the cameras."

"Maybe, but I have a feeling she's connected."

"Then I think we do both, but there's no coming back here. We'll have to prepare for sleeping rough for a while."

Deter shuddered at the thought of being on the run again, especially in the unpredictable British weather, but faced with the option of things continuing as they were, she felt she didn't have much choice.

They decided to wait until the 7th of April during the last night of *Cinderella*. Amongst the stage props they hid several rucksacks with spare clothes, food, battery packs and cash. No one in the cast or crew would bother rifling through the boxes, as they were all consumed by their own tasks for the imminent performances.

As Act 2 got underway for the final time, Deter left the wings, where Brian had just started engaging the audience in a participatory song, where things go 'bang, bang, bang, bangetty bang' and even 'bong, bong, bong, bongetty bong'.

Things had even started to go 'tra-la-la' as Brian drove a cardboard car 'fa-la-la' around the stage, when Lincoln and Deter slipped out the stage door with their packs on their backs. Two of the seven dwarves would be looking for their beards and hats later, as Lincoln had decided at the last minute that they would make great disguises.

They headed south over the river, crossing Tower Bridge and then following the river past the endless tourist attractions glorifying the darker side of London's history. Packed cafés and restaurants called to them to take a break, to enjoy the hot coffee and refuel, but Lincoln pushed them on at a swift pace, keen to be out of the Faction's home ground. At the Globe Theatre they couldn't help but stop to marvel at the timber-frame home of Shakespeare's plays. Originally owned by six actors, the building was now in its fourth reincarnation, having burnt down several times and also been pulled down in 1644 by Puritans who objected to the bawdy nature of the plays and the undesirables they attracted.

"We've been fighting over big and little things for years. We did think it would all end when FED hit. It united us all and then when the Establishment took over, we became a global community. It's all unravelling now, though," Lincoln reflected. "Maybe we can't help it, maybe it's in our nature."

They continued south, still following the river passing Westminster Bridge, and Lincoln began to relax a bit more as they reached the outskirts of Faction territory. He had no wish to be spotted by anyone from the Establishment either but felt safer knowing that Pip wouldn't sanction forcible retrieval so close to the Houses of Parliament. The Establishment had moved unquestioned into all the prominent buildings traditionally associated with power. No one had challenged it.

At Lambeth Bridge they debated which side of the river to stay on. Not knowing anything about either side of the Thames, they crossed over and followed Horseferry Road, which took them, unwittingly, into the heart of Westminster. It wasn't until they stumbled across the almost exotic stripes of the brick-patterned cathedral that they realised and hastily retreated south into Pimlico. Finding the nearest library in Lupus Street, Lincoln lost no time in linking up the monitor, while Deter grabbed much-needed refreshments.

It wasn't until they had nearly finished their hot chocolates that anything happened. On the bottom of their screen an innocuous, standard box popped up, saying 'live chat'. It could be any chat box, just like those for when your Internet banking goes wrong or your website crashes. Deter put her disposable cup down and leant forward, waiting.

It felt like forever, but after a few minutes a few dots appeared and flashed to indicate that someone was typing. It looked like they were typing a whole essay, but when the text finally arrived on their screen it was just a few lines.

"Don't be scared."

They looked at the writing, then at each other.

"OK, I'm sure that's meant to be reassuring, but it really kinda isn't," said Lincoln.

"What do we do? Shall we reply?"

Before they had time to consider, a new series of dots started flashing.

"Oh no, perhaps we should turn it off?" Deter fretted.

"Too late," said Lincoln as the next much longer message popped up.

"It's me, Amery. I've been looking for you. Are you all right?"

"No, it can't be! Amery?" Deter gasped in disbelief.

"So it says. Doesn't mean it is, though."

"We should at least reply." Hope rushed through Deter, making her dizzy.

"OK!" Lincoln typed three question marks into the box and pressed send.

They waited as the dots flashed again, then a much longer flow of text arrived.

"I understand. You are sensible to be wary. Please take a leap of faith, after all, nothing comes from nothing."

"It's her! It's definitely her. That's her motto, hardly a week went by without her saying it to me!"

"Really! OK, but let's be cautious. Let's ask questions without giving too much away."

During the next thirty minutes they established that Amery was on a remote island, which, unknown to the Establishment, was thriving and running successful businesses around the world. Amery had gone from being outcast to being highly valued, and had organised a search for her most precious girl. Deter took over the keyboard, as she and Amery had so much to ask each other, and she sobbed as she heard how Amery had never stopped thinking of her. Lincoln had to force more hot drinks down her to distract her, as her noisy nose blowing was attracting attention from the others in the library. The last thing they wanted was to be caught by the Establishment or the Faction during an emotional online reunion.

Before they severed the connection, it was arranged that a woman named Maria would meet them at the north side of Lambeth Bridge in half an hour. They would know her, as she would wear a bright red hat.

Before they left, Lincoln hesitated, then returned to the console.

Typing quickly, Lincoln set the computer to open a command prompt six times then continuously loop until the computer froze. Anyone now trying to track their conversation would have a terrible job just to get it to open.

"Don't worry, it hasn't damaged the computer, it will just slow them down, we just need a thirty-minute head start." He grinned.

"I don't think anyone is following us," said Deter, looking around at the studious library clientele.

"Maybe not, but you can't be too sure," muttered Lincoln darkly.

"Just admit it, you can't pass up an opportunity to show off your geeky prowess," Deter teased as they swung their backpacks up onto their shoulders and left the warm, cosy building for the sharp, cold night air.

MARIA

Maria was tired and so glad to be leaving London. It was a cramped and miserable place, and she missed home. She had agreed to take on this job purely for the money and now it was over she wanted to leave as quickly as she could.

Her latest orders were to charter a boat to meet Deter and Lincoln at Lambeth Bridge. There was a small, wooden jetty and already several other boats were tethered there. They were still waiting for a space to pull up when she saw a couple pointing to her red hat. She took the hat off and waved it in greeting. The couple made their way to the end of the jetty and then, encouraged by her waving, they walked across a small barge, which luckily didn't seem to have any occupants. They then jumped into the small motorboat with her.

Deter recognised her instantly, but Maria deflected her questions by ushering them aboard and saying tersely, "Yes, you've seen me before, long story."

She wasn't in the mood for chatting. The captain of their small vessel waited for her signal then pulled out and set off back the way Deter and Lincoln had come an hour ago. Maria didn't say much, so Lincoln and Deter settled down and enjoyed watching night-time London as they cruised past.

The black water caught the lights and white ripples rushed busily away from them out to sea. An orange haze surrounded the city, preventing it from ever being truly dark, and the stars they had enjoyed on their journey from New York were nowhere to be seen.

As they rounded the corner from Tower Bridge, the wind picked up, and Deter felt distinctly chilly as they hugged the north bank, aiming to dock at Canary Wharf pier. She and Lincoln sat as near together as they could, partly to keep warm and partly to shield each other from Maria's hostile expression. Before they had time to collect their thoughts, Maria hastily ushered them off the boat and, despite having a million questions, they only had to look at her to keep their mouths shut. She seemed intent on her mission and they did their best to keep up.

Maria had nothing against either Lincoln or Deter, but the longer they were in her care, the longer she had to wait for payment, and all she wanted was to get back to Selina.

They paused by a large ex-military ship that loomed over them while Maria looked for the boat organised by Amery. The boat was registered to one of the wealthiest American inventors, whose private vessel could move around the world without any questions, as the trillionaire owner was a revered benefactor of the Establishment. It was sheer luck that it was moored up here.

Don Carlos Black put his money into many ventures and had just injected a further six billion into research at the Establishment for the new cure. He specialised in what he called 'Essential Solutions', in other words things people couldn't live without. From customised air to purified water, he made it his business to bring faster and safer access to these commodities worldwide. He was also one of the biggest investors in the work by the Sanctum, pioneers in organ and limb transplants, for the boats they used as floating hospitals couldn't operate without his financial support. His newest obsession was developing a new fungus to break down corpses to render them useful and to recycle them into the food chain. The FED crisis had led to immediate problems with body disposal, and burial was limited as land space was becoming more and more precious as water levels rose. Cremation, although a short-term solution, seemed to him a waste. The fungi he developed broke the tissue into useable compost that destroyed the virus so that all food grown was completely harmless. Almost every community now had their own compost area full of Black's fungi. Known to be tough on his children, he didn't give them more than the usual basic allowance and insisted that anything they wanted they had to work for. His generosity to his causes, however, was unlimited.

Shimmering into visibility, a sleek and stealthy luxury yacht appeared before them and a black gangplank with purple lights was slowly lowered. Maria went ahead to talk to a figure in the shadows while they hovered on the walkway feeling awkward and staring into the water as it glowed hypnotically.

"You will be taken to your friend. The journey will last a few weeks, but everything you need is on board. The crew will care for you, but I'm afraid you will be travelling alone as your friend is not expected."

Maria looked at Deter apologetically but gestured firmly for her to get on board.

"No, I can't leave Lincoln here. He has nowhere to go. The Faction won't trust him after the way we left tonight. We are on this journey together."

Totally stricken with fear for Lincoln and for her own sanity without him, Deter was plunged into confusion. The journey from her safe and naïve past life into this hellish reality had only been made manageable thanks to his kindness and willingness to guide her. She hadn't imagined that this would happen when they made the decision to leave and if she had, she never would have gone.

"It's only just gone midnight. If you return now," Maria turned to Lincoln, whose pale face reflected ghostly mauve; tiredness and shock made him seem more skeletal than ever and she felt a twinge of sympathy, "no one will know you've gone, and you can say that you went running after Deter and that you couldn't find her."

"No, he must come too," Deter sobbed. "Lincoln, I can't leave you."

"Deter, you must. There's no time for us to think, we must just do as planned. Amery loves you and we must trust her. You can't stay here, there are too many questions and I'll be safe. Pip is a good guy and I'll explain everything to him."

As they embraced, Deter's tears dropped on to Lincoln's hand and they burnt hot against his cold skin. She was trying to give him something, but it took him a while to work out what she was doing and he nearly dropped it. Trying to conceal it, he tried not to look down, keeping his focus on her beautiful face.

"You should know..." he began. "Just in case—"

She stopped him with her lips and then, drawing back, she smiled a devastatingly sad smile as she whispered, "As beautiful as your goodbye speech would be, there simply isn't time. I know. I love you too."

Resting her hand on his heart, she could see the faint glow of his chest through her fingers.

She turned and walked up the gangway, leaving Maria and Lincoln on the dock. As the boat pulled away, a cold draft of air whipped round them and Lincoln, straining his eyes to catch a final glimpse of her, thought his ravaged heart would break.

ROLLER

Roller became separated from Phib and Aaron quite early on. He could see Barney just ahead of him, who had raised himself up on his personal platform and was being propelled forward by the surging crowd. Roller regretted his wheels for the first time and wished he had extending legs to give him height over the masses of people gathered for the march.

It was extraordinary how support had gathered, even from those who had seemed so content. Little gripes, such as the price of seeds and restrictions on trading livestock, had brought the farmers down from their secluded green world in the sky. Plus, almost everyone knew someone who had been persuaded to 'donate' a limb. Stories grew more dramatic and sensational with each mile that they gained on the city, Margaret herself happily elaborating on how she was 'forced' to give up her arm in exchange for a fancy new prosthetic leg. Yes, they had played on her desperation and vulnerability. Wasn't it terrible? The itching and slight swelling on her new stump, now vastly exaggerated into unbearable phantom pain and threat of infection. Strangers put their arms around her and tutted in sympathy and raised their arms in solidarity against their wealthy oppressors. The overall experience had actually been nothing but positive for Margaret: new leg and enough funds for a high-tech new arm in the future too. She couldn't fault the care she had received from the Sanctum from the first time that Maria approached her, to the aftercare that she was still secretly receiving. All her debt had now been cleared and on top of that, she was centre of attention and very happy to play the victim. Raising her voice, she happily joined in the chanting: "People wake up, our lives, our bodies."

There was an irritating delay as crowds bottle-necked on the approach to Manhattan Bridge until a brief lull in traffic saw a brave group storm the highway. This led to confusion as parties were split up, but new comrades were made and the march continued. Despite the numbers, there was only one casualty, and the young man was quickly lifted out and driven ahead of his fellow campaigners by the very car that knocked him down.

It wasn't the quickest route, but they picked up support from Lower Manhattan and East Village as they passed by. After four hours and the seemingly never-ending FDR, their spirits were sagging. A timely boost to morale came as thousands more people poured out of Queens Midtown Tunnel to join them up 42nd Street towards Times Square. Roller fell in line with another group of young men with blue shirts emblazoned with 'Astoria Big Apples' on their chests; they were waving a huge banner saying, 'Where's our balls?'

"Yo momma give you apples instead of balls?" Roller sniggered.

"Wish she had, then we wouldn't be hungry." One of the boys clapped his hand on Roller's shoulders good-naturedly.

"Nice wheels!"

"Thanks," Roller grinned, "Nice shirts!"

"Yeah! Bit of a giveaway where we're from. But we're proud of our team."

"We've been asking the Establishment for help with running costs for years. Not just balls, but kit, insurance, pitch hire… all that shiz."

Roller didn't know much about sport, as no one he knew played any. "Thought you had support from businesses?"

"Not many businesses can afford it these days."

"Not many businesses left," another kid chipped in.

"Especially not now business rates have doubled."

Roller felt even more ignorant. "I didn't know they had. Not many enterprises where we are."

A large woman barging through with her 'Down with the Establishment' banner interrupted them. She held one end and a small girl clung to the other as her mother pulled her onwards.

'Down with the Establishment', still ringing in their ears, the boys exchanged glances briefly before a tidal wave of people ran through the mob, dividing them up. This new wave came from the right as the official chant came up around them: "People wake up, our lives, our bodies." As a fresh tide of hollering and hot limbs swept around him, Roller realised these were the much-hoped-for hoards from Harlem. Angus had said he prayed they would join them, and it looked like his prayers had been answered. There were so many of them that they stretched along 7th Avenue and back up into Central Park, although some of them had been distracted from their purpose and were eating chips on the steps of the Metropolitan, their banners crumpled next to them.

Roller couldn't see anyone he knew, not even his new footballing friends, so he pushed his way to the side and climbed up cautiously onto a stationary bus. The first thing he did was check his phone, but the battery had died. *Great!* He should have turned it off during the walk. He checked his battery pack, but it was low, so he weighed up the urgency of the situation and decided to keep what reserves he had for an emergency.

Looking out at the crowd, he felt immediately uplifted. The sea of protestors was incredible, and he gave out a loud cry, whooping with the excitement of it all. He felt pride and deep affinity with his people that ran through his belly and set his heart pounding. Nothing like this had ever happened before. The Brownsville community had pretty much cocooned themselves for at least three generations, dealing with death, disease and poverty without expecting anything from outsiders. They were self-sufficient and sustained by their own endeavours and religion. But when people started coming in and stirring up unrest and making them feel they were somehow 'less', then those people would learn not to mess with Brownsville. *And what a lesson! Look at the support from other communities!*

Still not seeing anyone he knew, he climbed down, cursing his wheels, which slid on the bonnet. He was tired and they still hadn't made it to Times Square. Letting the tide carry him along, he allowed himself to be propelled up 42nd Street. At Bryant Park he was relieved to recognise Angus's voice over a loudspeaker, rallying the crowd, and every now and again the crowd responded, chanting, "People wake up, our lives, our bodies."

Roller tried to reach Angus, as he could see Barney nearby. Barney was a brilliant landmark, towering over everyone. Just as Angus's speech seemed to be winding down, there was a new ripple of unease spreading through the crowd. People were muttering about the Establishment responding aggressively.

Apparently, Angus had been recognised as a former Faction leader and the Establishment had sent troops to detain him. Angus seemed unaware of the impending danger and Roller needed to warn him as quickly as possible.

Frantically looking round for someone, anyone, that he knew, Roller finally saw Aaron and Phib. They were right next to Barney but tucked behind a tree so he hadn't seen them until now. He gestured wildly to them, but they didn't see. Luckily Barney did and waved back.

"Warn Angus!" he shouted, pointing to Angus urgently.

Barney shrugged as he couldn't hear, and took his phone and gestured to it.

Roller shook his head and mouthed, "It's dead!"

Barney shrugged again and, despite Roller shouting and waving, he turned away from Roller to watch the end of Angus's speech.

It was a race to see who got to Angus first as Roller saw no option but to carve a way through the crowd himself. But flanking him was a line of the Establishment's soldiers. They were ploughing through the protestors to get to the speaker. Luckily, the angry mob didn't take kindly to being pushed out of the way, as the Establishment's representatives were the last people they wanted to see. Roller was making good progress and could also see that Barney had finally cottoned on to what was happening.

"About time!" he shouted as he pushed his way towards them.

What happened next happened quickly, but to Roller it seemed as though time was held suspended. There were several loud explosions and everyone was screaming. The sound was overwhelming and there was too much movement as panic hit the crowd. Roller ducked down and shut his eyes. He tried to get back up again, but he couldn't gain a foothold as his wheels slid against other flailing limbs. Breathing became difficult and there was a thudding in his ear, which made it hard to orientate himself. Someone had lost a leg and it flew through the air and hit Roller on the shoulder. Recovering, he finally stood up in time to see a soldier reach out to grab Angus, but in a swift move, Angus evaded capture by stepping to the side. This had a knock-on effect, as Aaron had been about to cuff the soldier but instead found Angus in the way. To avoid hitting Angus, he jerked his elbow back, knocking into Phib, who, caught off-balance, cannoned into Barney. Still being at his extended height, Barney was easy to tip over. It would have been a classic slapstick sketch if it had been performed on stage, but watching helplessly stranded amongst the terrified crowd, Roller found it agonising, as the scene ended with Barney tipping into the pond and no one being able to help him as they were fending off their own assailants.

In the end, Angus managed to escape, but Aaron and Phib were arrested. By the time Roller managed to get to Barney, he wasn't moving. The fall had knocked him out, but even if he'd been conscious, he wouldn't have been able to escape as the weight of his own chair would have held him down under the water. Roller realised that Barney was dead. Full of grief and anger, Roller allowed himself to collapse next to his friend. Carefully lifting Barney's face out of the water, he held him, cradling him, not knowing what to do next. Roller lay there, suspended in this terrible moment in time, until the gentle hands of his Brownsville family lifted them both and carried them home.

"He's just a kid," someone said sadly. "They are all just kids."

Barney was one of fifty-two who died at the peaceful demonstrations that day. Fear over Angus's involvement had led to a heavy-handed approach by the Establishment. They had been wondering if there were any survivors from the three top pods in New York and now they knew. Angus was still out there and even though he wasn't armed, he was fast becoming the most dangerous man they knew.

MARIA

The Establishment's persecution of Angus ended up by bringing more support for the Faction. Until the protest, not many people knew who Angus was. Now, with his fame spreading, unrest was growing internationally. Those who died that day became martyrs to the cause and the Establishment was losing support daily.

Support for the cause had spread by word of mouth and secret bulletins, and the size and scale of it surprised everyone. Now they knew that they had an ex-Faction soldier who had laid down his arms for a peaceful and modest life with the Brownsville community, support grew even bigger.

Aline walked about with a serene smile on her face as her prediction had come true. She thanked God every day for bringing Angus to them and prayed for his safety. No one knew where Angus was hiding, but the whole neighbourhood was proud of the role they had played in what they saw as the start on the war against the privileged ruling classes. They went into extended mourning for Barney; his body was laid on the bed for all to pay homage. An unsettling mix of anticlimax and anticipation hung heavy on them all, as they asked themselves and each other, what next? How far do we go? How do we actually want to see change implemented?

None of this interested or affected Maria. She only had one concern, and that was Selina.

As soon as the boat carrying Deter to the Kerguelen Islands pulled out of Canary Wharf, she slipped out of sight, leaving Lincoln on his own, staring into the dark river.

Swiftly and efficiently, she embarked on another of Black's private boats for passage back to New York. This was one of the floating hospitals for the Sanctum and the journey would have two purposes: one, to take her back to Selina and two, to fit her with a new prosthetic leg. Once she landed, she would never work with Marcus again and would never need to, having earnt enough to ensure her little family could live comfortably for the rest of their lives. She had been amazed by how easy it had been to sign people up for both limb and organ donation. Money really did talk, especially to people who had so little. Bonny had been one of the first to sign up and once she started spreading the news to her friends, Maria had a pretty constant flow of people interested. Plus, by following her carefully thought-out plan of three circles – close friends, acquaintances and vulnerable groups – she had grown enough contacts to supply her with future leads without too much effort. Marcus had been really impressed.

She might see if Bonny wanted to take over her side of the business, as she couldn't bear to hand her contacts over to Marcus. She could offer it to Bonny with the proviso that she retained a percentage. After all, it didn't hurt to have regular funds coming in. She looked out of the circular window as the lights of the docklands became smaller and smaller, and imagined Selina's excitement if she were with her. *We'll be going on our own holidays soon*, she thought; she couldn't wait. *That'll show Ian and his snotty new wife.*

The journey was long and forced Maria to take stock of her current situation. Her relationship with Andy had ended before it had really restarted as there was too much history, and he was absolutely disgusted by her new job. She had to tell him, as despite making initial progress, Selina had been rushed back into hospital with suspected encephalitis. This had forced her to step up her recruitment programme a notch.

"Nothing, and no amount of money, can justify this," he had roared angrily when she'd finally confided in him. "Surely with my income we would have enough?"

"Enough to carry on muddling through!" she had shouted back. "I want more than enough. More than cooking, cleaning and miniature railways can bring in," she had raged. "I've spent too many years working three jobs just to make ends meet and it's time things turned around. Here is the perfect opportunity."

"But it is so wrong!" he had exploded. "On all levels. Who are these ridiculous people paying to have limb transplants? Isn't it enough that some people are dying and *need* to have organ transplants without making a mockery of the whole process? It's a lifesaving procedure, not a cosmetic one."

"Who cares? I do not have to see them or deal with them, the people I see are the ones like me, who have the chance to make some serious difference in their lives."

"At a cost," Andy had spat back.

"We've already lost so many parts of our bodies, it's nothing," she had retorted angrily. "FED took my leg without my permission, and at least I give people a choice."

He had looked disgusted and chillingly disappointed. "The bits I still have, I value and treasure. They are the precious parts of me that don't require daily maintenance."

"That's how these rich people feel! The joy of a pain-free body, imagine being as close to being Complete as possible, without anyone thinking you're weird or freaky. Bonus!" she had countered.

Andy had scowled. "I don't know how you can live with yourself. It's all right going into it with clear choices, knowing your rights and understanding what you're agreeing to. But there are loads of people who won't feel they have a choice. Making that choice for yourself is one thing, but encouraging others is another. That's called exploitation!"

"You make it sound as though I'm nothing short of evil. Thanks for the support," Maria had hissed.

Well, that had been a while ago, and Maria had kissed her sleeping Selina goodbye, leaving enough funds behind to pay for top-level care while she was away. She had been incredibly grateful to Marcus, who'd offered her the highly secret and sensitive job in London. She felt like she had won a Willy Wonka golden ticket!

The Sanctum had offered her a ridiculously large fee to find a girl called Deter Edison. They had been monitoring her remotely for nearly eighteen years but lost sight of her. Maria was interested to see that she was the Immune that everyone had been talking about a while ago. She hadn't paid that much attention until now. The Sanctum had undercover agents worldwide who were looking for her, and they thought they had spotted her in London. They needed someone discreet, reliable, with the ability to blend in. They wanted someone not already in the field, as they didn't want to compromise years of existing work. Training in surveillance would be given on the journey over. Maria leapt at the chance, as it would help keep her busy instead of fretting over her daughter and get her away from Andy. However, now her task was complete, Deter had been found and was now on her way across the sea, Maria could allow herself to focus entirely on her own needs.

She leant back, enjoying the softness of the robe that had been left out for her and allowed the masseuse to gently ease the last few weeks' tension from her shoulders and neck.

Exhaling, Maria pushed all negative thoughts away and smiled with the sudden realisation that she could not only get used to this life but could actually now afford it.

LINCOLN

Lincoln hesitated; he reached out to open the door but stopped to think things through.

He was not only tired but also completely empty inside. Deter was gone. There was nothing for him here; there was nothing without her.

It had taken him longer to walk back than anticipated as his thoughts were flying across the sea, and every now and then he stumbled into dead ends. He cursed the narrow, unpredictable roads and wished for the big, wide, obvious streets at home. He didn't even care whether Pip caught him coming back in, but he knew it would be foolish to alienate his only allies.

His plan was to slip into bed, wake as usual and then pretend that Deter had vanished without his knowledge. It wasn't the best plan; everyone would have noticed they both were missing after the show. He would have to come up with some excuse as to why they didn't attend the aftershow party.

Plus, there were the missing dwarves' costumes to explain. Damn, he was never going to get away with this.

He finally clicked the lock and opened the creaky old door. *Why do British people insist on keeping ancient buildings in such rickety states?* He could hear his heart beating as he negotiated the tell-tale floorboards on the uneven corridor. Nearly there… he'd made it! Feeling a sense of relief that he could finally rest, he didn't even bother to check his prosthetics, even though he could tell the long day was going to have repercussions.

He fell asleep quicker than he thought and despite the day's trauma, he slept deeply and dreamlessly.

Suddenly, the door banged open and a loud, cheery voice startled him awake. "It's good to know you're alive and well! Where've you been?" Martha swept in, enveloped in a huge, floral dressing gown and seeing just Lincoln, she frowned. "Where's Deter? Don't tell me you've had a falling out? I knew something must have happened as you missed the aftershow party! What was it about? Couldn't you have chosen a better time to have a domestic?"

"Um…" Lincoln sat up, completely disorientated and trying to catch up with Martha's quick-fire questions. He pushed up his sleeves and tried to smooth his bedhead into something vaguely respectable. "I have to say, my head isn't feeling great today. I should have stopped after the third gin and tonic, but for some reason, it seemed such a good idea to finish the bottle."

Uninvited, Martha flopped down and lay on the bed next to Lincoln who froze both out of embarrassment and panic.

"Um…" He started to speak again, not entirely sure what he was going to follow 'um' with, but luckily he was interrupted again.

"Don't tell me, she was fretting about her imaginary stalker again, wasn't she? You don't have to lie; I know all about it.

Everyone's noticed she's so jumpy when we are out and about and anyway, I heard you talking about it in the costume storeroom."

Lincoln tried desperately to remember a conversation that could have been overheard but couldn't think of anything, let alone something that specific. He thought they'd kept the fact she was being followed completely secret. Still, Martha was giving him a perfect story to go along with. It made sense that they were having some private time to sort out their issues. Without him even trying, things were going according to plan, thanks to Martha.

"Well, you'd better finish sorting it out today, as no one wants grumpy faces on today's shift. Deter's with me this lunchtime and I can't cope with her sad face when I have the hangover from hell."

Lincoln looked at the time... it was late. Usually he was one of the first to arrive at the research institute; if he skipped breakfast, he might avoid being one of the last.

"I'm sorry, Martha, I've overslept. Pip's easygoing, but his uncle isn't, so I've got to dash." He leapt up, expecting her to move and give him some space, but she opened her eyes and glared at him.

"It's Sunday, you moron! Oh my God, your head must be worse than mine." Martha shut her eyes and draped her hand over her forehead dramatically.

Help! He really wasn't with it today, and he needed all his wits about him. "I'm going to see if Deter's awake, maybe we could get some breakfast?" He hoped he sounded normal. He wished he had Pip and Brian's acting skills, because now he had to go to Deter's room, pretending they'd had a row, but knowing full well that not only was there no row, but there was also no Deter.

He knocked at Deter's door and pushed it open, saying brightly, "It's me," to the empty room. He paused, pretending to look behind the door. *Oh my God,* he thought, *who looks behind doors? I'm so glad no one's watching.*

He made his way back to the inert Martha, who looked like she'd fallen asleep.

"Um…" He coughed. "Um… she's not in her room."

Martha looked cross at being disturbed. "Well, maybe she's gone out or already having breakfast somewhere. Not everyone wants to look at your stupid face when they're eating."

"Er… OK." Unsure what to do next and keen to have some time to himself, he grabbed some clean clothes and went off to wash. He peeled one prosthetic arm off at a time and rubbed his sore stump. Without them both on, Lincoln felt unbalanced and only half a person. Sometimes, if he looked at himself too closely, he could feel a deep sadness threatening to creep in. What a world, what a desperate situation mankind was in. After his shower, he took the monitor from his pocket and opened it, gently caressing the miniature city.

This tiny ceramic ornament was the only link he now had with Deter. It was an important symbolic memento of their time together and how this crazy adventure together had started. It was also the only possible communication link that they had. He pushed it back into his jeans and hoped that no one would notice it. He'd need to find a decent hiding place for it as soon as Martha had left his room.

Once dressed, he mustered up what strength he had to face what he knew would be unfolding throughout the day. He could do this. He could pretend Deter left him without a word; in fact if he could convince himself to start believing it, he would find her loss so much easier to cope with.

JOSEPH

Confident that his researchers were making progress with developing a new cure, Professor Joseph meticulously folded his clothes and laid them neatly in piles, ready to transfer to his suitcase.

He had streamlined funds to be attributed to three avenues of research, all interdependent and none of greater priority than the other. The first, the new cure, would of course have the most popular support and be of greatest value to the investors, but only on an altruistic level, as they had promised fully funded and subsidised doses would be issued to the masses. It would, of course, ensure continued public support for the Establishment, but at quite a high financial cost. These funds he hoped would be recouped though the discovery of a way to reverse the horrendous side effects of the last cure.

Cure correction, this second avenue of research, would satisfy high-profile investors such as the Poppes and Lithgows, consolidate the relationship they had with them and ensure that the human race survived into the next generation. There would be enough people willing to pay for this to ensure their lineage continues, to claw back lost revenue.

Lastly, and more privately, the professor refused to give up his dream of breeding a naturally immune super race. Not having the Edison girl was a blow, but he had plans to concentrate on the small community in Italy. The community they had planned to send Deter to. By manipulating genetics, he hoped to increase the number of naturally immune.

But this would of course, all take time. It looked as though it would certainly be time worth investing in, now that the cloning programme was proving a failure. To further his knowledge and to discuss collaboration, Professor Joseph was preparing to travel to see the leaders of the Sanctum.

If it hadn't been for one of his investors, Don Black, he might not have thought of contacting them, but he understood that they had made substantial progress in areas that the Establishment would never be allowed to sanction. For it seemed that the Sanctum were conducting interesting experiments at a long-forgotten site in the remote Kerguelen Islands. Black had kindly set up introductions and now here he was, about to leave for the remotest part of the world.

What was even more exciting was that one of the Sanctum's own boats was taking him there, and the month-long trip would be spent observing the lead surgeon and having the latest procedures explained to him. He felt a mix of excitement and jealousy, as it was galling to think that someone else was leading the way with research. However, links with the Sanctum had been established over a hundred years ago, and although the Establishment involvement had lapsed in the past few decades, he would ensure that their glory was also his glory.

Satisfied that he had thought of everything, he transferred his immaculate piles of clothes to his travel case, and fastidiously secured the lid.

The journey was incredible. The medical personnel on board were all too delighted to demonstrate new procedures that he hadn't even thought possible, and he was amazed at the numbers of willing donors on their records. The pre-care and aftercare was as high as the actual standard of mid-operation care and he was seriously considering having his own leg and arm replaced with donor limbs. In fact, maybe he could spend his return journey as a patient?

Dr Tony Armitage had been so welcoming, and Joseph appreciated the surgeon's deference to the professor's status. Nothing riled him more than young doctors who assumed they knew more than him and talked in patronising tones as though he was too old to be taken seriously. The time on board passed all too quickly, and the professor's notebook bulged with excited scribblings.

As the ship finally weighed anchor, a smaller boat was making its way to greet them. It was a grey day, with spray shooting high into the air and seeming to never come back down but instead hung as a fine mist, coating anyone foolish enough to be standing outdoors. The rocks were too dangerous for the floating hospital to come any closer, and Joseph stood on the deck with the crew, watching the small taxi's progress. It was a little choppy and most of his fellow travellers were inside, enjoying some serious rest and relaxation, safe from the corrosive sea breeze.

He pulled his hat down further over his ears and carefully stepped aboard the small motorboat.

DETER

There was a huge ship, almost as big as the island itself, white and imposing against the bleak sky. It had arrived at the same time as her boat, but Deter couldn't see inside it as they were too far away. Her small, nippy craft neatly negotiated the rocks and other islands as they headed towards a large, low building, as dark as the volcanic rock it was built on.

She could see another small boat with several passengers from the ship heading for the same small jetty. She pulled her hoodie up and held her hands over her ears as the wind was slicing through and it wasn't very pleasant. She squinted, wiping salty droplets from her eyes, trying to see if Amery was outside waiting to greet her, but each time she wiped, more water ran persistently down her face. As they drew nearer, she saw with certainty a small, familiar figure looking out for her. She sobbed with relief and hugged her arms around herself tightly to keep herself from falling apart.

AMERY

It was a typically dark day and a gust of damp debris flew up around her, compromising her vision, but she was sure she could see Deter stumbling towards her. There were several other passengers and crew making their way towards the only building offering respite in this bleak landscape. She hurried forward towards Deter, her arms outstretched. A man tripped as she rushed past and she reached out to steady him, as he seemed a little older than their usual visitors.

"Careful sir, you don't want to spend your visit here in plaster." Amery smiled.

Looking more carefully, Amery realised with a shock that under his hat this man was familiar. Too familiar.

"Amery, I can't believe it's you!" Deter had reached them and had flung her arms around Amery, clasping her tightly with every ounce of love and affection she had.

"No, I can't either," said the old man drily.

"Deter, it's wonderful to see you." Amery kissed her distractedly, not able to take her eyes off the old man. "Hello, Dad, I wish I could say the same for you."

ACKNOWLEDGMENTS

It was hard to make that jump from writing in secret to being open about it. I couldn't have managed without my family and friends who received the news with genuine delight and interest.

The very first person to read 'Measure of Days' was my niece and goddaughter Isabel Denny who sent me a series of encouraging shooting star emojis! Her positive reaction gave me the confidence to share it more widely and I'm very grateful to everyone who read the first draft and gave me their reviews and comments. In particular I would like to mention Joanne Crocker, Beccy Swaine, Karen Roberts, Ella Wall, Lindsay Dumble, Karin Cumming, Marika Sterry and Jane Watkins who all took the time to talk to me and gave me useful feedback. Most importantly, you gave me confidence, thank you.

I am also enormously grateful to The Book Guild for their hard work bringing this book to fruition; you have all been marvellous to work with. Thank you so much for believing in me.

Lastly, to my daughter Amelia who this book is for and who I admire hugely for her courage and stoicism and to my husband for encouraging me to indulge all my creative pursuits.

Sophy
www.sophylayzell.com